Finding Atlantis

J.M. Dover

You are stronger than you think

J.M. D—

EVIL ALTER EGO PRESS

www.evilalteregopress.wordpress.com

Evil Alter Ego Press

www.evilalteregopress.wordpress.com

Published by Evil Alter Ego Press, 869 Citadel Drive NW, Calgary, AB T3G 4B8, Canada

Finding Atlantis, Copyright © 2018 by JM Dover.

Edited by Jeffrey A. Hite and Barbara Jacobson.

Cover by Jeff Minkevics, copyright © 2018 by Jeff Minkevics.

Interior design and layout by Michell Plested.

Print version set in Cambria; titles in Cambria, byline in Cambria.

Published in Canada

Printed in Canada

Library and Archives Canada Cataloguing in Publication

Dover, J.M., 1960-, author

Finding Atlantis / J.M. Dover.

Electronic monograph issued in EPUB and print format.

ISBN 978-1-988361-12-3 (pbk.).
ISBN 978-1-988361-13-0 (epub).

Contents

For my mother, who gave me the gift of stories,
and for Dan, who inspired me to bring my stories to life.

Chapter One

The vortex of swirling water sucked Adam deeper into the ocean. His heart pounded in his ears as he thrashed against the force of the turbulence, but his actions did nothing to stop the downward spiral. Above him, the deep turquoise water spun in sickening circles. Below him, a pinpoint of light grew slowly bigger as he was drawn toward it. What was happening?

Adam's stomach clenched. If only he hadn't argued with his dad.

"You can go to the beach later." Dad turned from setting the table and eyed his swimming trunks. "You're supposed to be helping your sisters clean up."

"But Dad..."

"No," his father said in a firm voice.

There was no way he would help his sisters clean up a mess he hadn't created. The angry words had flown out of his mouth. "You don't know how I feel. You don't care. You're not even my real dad." He'd run out of the house, slamming the door behind him.

As soon as his bare feet hit the soft Caribbean sand, he'd regretted his words. His dad would always be his dad, even if he was adopted.

Then the white sand squished between his toes, sending a sensation like a gentle surge of electric current flowing into his feet. The warm vibration moved up his legs and through his body. He sighed, like he always did, when the feeling reached his brain. He didn't understand why he had these strange feelings, but for a fleeting moment he was connected to the universe, and the rest of the world didn't matter. If he didn't have these weird feelings, he wouldn't have ended up here, now. Wherever here was.

If he'd stayed out of the water that would've worked too, but the waves lapping on the shore whispered his name. Snorkelling. He could watch the fish playing beneath the waves, if he had his mask and fins.

Something rubbery touched his fingers, a familiar weight. He glanced down to see his snorkelling equipment dangling from his left hand. Weird. He didn't remember grabbing them, but perhaps he'd done that when he stormed out of the house. He should have known then, that something wasn't right.

His mother always said, 'Don't go into the water by yourself''. Maybe if he'd listened to her sensible advice, then he wouldn't be here. No one else was on the beach, so he thought he was safe because no one would tell her what he'd done.

Stepping into the ocean, the cool water surged around his feet. The swish of the waves drowned out the sound of his mother's voice, and called to him, drawing him like a magnet to a piece of iron.

He'd just swim for a few minutes. Close to shore. He knew he shouldn't have done it, but he somehow couldn't stop himself.

Then he slipped the fins onto his feet, adjusted the mask on his face and backed into the water. When the ocean came up to his waist, he turned and floated face down, kicking his legs to propel himself into the surf.

Gazing into the clear water, he saw the tropical fish darting about below him. His father joked that Adam liked snorkelling so much because he lured the fish to him, and they followed him wherever he swam. A flash of yellow with black stripes swam past. An angelfish. In a crevice on the brain coral, a bright blue tang nibbled at algae. A colourful parrot fish played around the red fan coral.

He caught a flash of movement out of the corner of his eye. An orange fish with bright blue stripes darted away from him. Adam had never seen a fish like that before. It disappeared for a moment, then popped up further away. The other fish chased after the small fish as if they were playing a game.

Adam dived down for a better look. He almost caught up when, again, the little fish dove out of sight. Swimming to the point where he last saw it, he paused at the edge of a small ridge. He'd never swam that deep before.

When he looked up, the surface had glittered far away. His heart flipped in his chest. The blue tang nudged his hand and swam toward the little fish, encouraging him to follow. The parrot fish did the same thing. All the fish watched him as if they were expecting him to come with them.

He couldn't. He wouldn't be able to breathe. Adam glanced up at the surface again, not sure what to do. Then he realized he hadn't been holding his breath, and he hadn't run out of air. How could that be possible? He closed his eyes, inhaled deeply, and... oxygen filled his lungs. Warm water cocooned him and a rush of familiar energy filled his body. The ocean had answered, and he no longer questioned it.

When he opened his eyes, he saw two large stone statues below him. Lions, with wings on their backs. Each with a front paw resting on a globe. The regal creatures stood guard at the sides of a massive gate made of iron bars. The gate sat by itself among the corals.

The colourful fish swam through the gate, then turned to look at Adam, as if daring him to catch up. Adam plunged toward the fish.

His hand brushed the gate, and the ocean had swirled around him.

Chapter Two

Adam's feet hit solid ground and his vision cleared. He stood on a cobblestone street looking at a row of ancient grey stone buildings. The sounds of people drifted to him from somewhere in the city, but here, he saw no one. His breath caught in his throat.

Overhead, a dazzling blue sky. How could he be deep underwater and see blue sky above? He turned. The underwater gate he had touched stood in the middle of a tall granite wall. Beyond it the deep ocean he had been swimming in only a moment ago could be seen through the gate, held back from spilling through the bars by nothing he could see. What kind of crazy place was this? This couldn't be real. The lack of oxygen must be making him see things.

Adam couldn't change the fact he'd touched the gate, even if it was by accident, but he had to find a way out of here. He reached up for his mask. His mask wasn't there. Had he lost it when he went through the gate?

Oh no!

His hands patted down his body, and it felt warm and dry. His swim suit had disappeared too. Instead, he wore a cream-coloured tunic and pajama-like pants.

A cold sweat formed on his back. What was happening?

He had to get home. He stomped toward the gate.

Behind him a voice announced, "The gate only opens one way."

Adam whirled around.

A boy with shaggy blond hair, who looked a couple of years

older than him, stood at the entrance to a narrow lane, scowling at him. He wore the same flowing clothing as Adam, but Adam felt like a skinny kid next to the boy's long-limbed body and wide shoulders.

"Who are you?" The boy squinted at him as if what he saw didn't add up.

Adam didn't have time for this. He rushed to the gate and hunted for a handle.

"You're..." The boy's voice curled in surprise. "You didn't come here through that gate."

Yes, I did, Adam thought. He couldn't find a latch on the gate.

"No one comes in through that gate."

"I did!" Adam shot the words at him. Could he climb the wall and get back into the water that way? But he had no mask or shorts.

"Once you enter the city, you can't go back." The boy's voice whispered. "Who...? Who *are* you?"

Maybe if Adam told him his name, the boy would tell him how to get out of this place. "My name is Adam. Adam Danburg," he said, in a voice shakier than he wanted.

The boy turned pale, and Adam didn't know why. "Come with me," he said abruptly. "I'll take you to the temple to see Noor." He showed the way with a gesture.

Adam fisted his hands at his sides. "Who are you, anyway? And why should I follow you?"

The boy raised an eyebrow. "I'm Orri." He studied Adam for a long moment, as if trying to decide what to do. "It's not my place to tell you what is going on," he said finally, "but you can't go back through the gate, so you might as well follow me."

No way. Adam pivoted back to the gate. His dad would be mad. His family...? Would he ever see them again? He rattled the bars like a prisoner trapped in a cell.

Nothing happened.

He pushed against it, straining to force it open until his arms ached and his heart pounded.

The gate didn't move.

He kicked the gate. Pain shot up his leg and he hopped

around holding his foot.

The gate remained solidly in place.

"Are you finished?" sneered Orri. "You can follow me or stay here. I don't care." He turned and walked away.

Watching Orri's retreating back, Adam considered having one more kick at the gate. His foot throbbed. He scanned the wall, looking for any chink he could use as a handhold, but the wall was smooth and unclimbable. He turned back and Orri was gone.

What now? The boy hadn't seemed very welcoming, but he'd at least offered to take Adam to someone who might help. Adam sprinted around the corner of a building to look for him.

A scattering of people walked on the road and its adjoining alleys, as if everything here was normal. They wore the same style of tunics and loose pants he had on, but in many different colours. He spotted Orri up ahead, striding down the cobbles. Adam ran after him.

The boy's gaze flicked down at him and he smirked briefly, but he didn't slow down.

Adam jogged to keep up with Orri's determined pace. They walked up a wide cobblestone road flanked by two- and three-story buildings made of brick and stone. This city seemed really old. It reminded Adam of a trip to Rome he'd taken with his parents, except there were no cars here.

Adam couldn't explain it, but somehow, he knew the weird sensations he felt when he touched nature had landed him in this bizarre place.

They crossed a low stone bridge over a curved canal. Here the crowds were thicker and hampered their passage. Some of the people they passed in the street stopped and stared at him. A few of them murmured, "Son of Earth," as he passed. One man commented excitedly to his companion, "I do believe that's Adam, Son of Earth."

Adam stared back. "How does he know my name?"

Orri scowled but didn't stop. "Your appearance is not unexpected. You'll have answers when we get to the Temple of Nethuns."

Not...not unexpected? What?

Orri suddenly turned into a tight alley where narrow houses leaned toward each other almost touching at the top. The empty lane twisted and turned like a squirming snake and the narrow strip of sky above didn't let in enough light to banish the deep shadows.

Adam's mouth went dry. "Where are you really taking me?" He hoped he didn't sound as scared as he felt.

Orri stopped. "I'm taking you to the temple." He turned around and shrugged. "Look, it's better if people don't recognize you, because..." He sighed. "It's complicated. Noor will explain everything much better than I can. Come on. The temple's not far. Trust me." He continued walking up the alley at a slower pace.

Trust him? It's complicated? Was he kidding? Adam's steps faltered. Maybe he could get back to the gate and find some way to get through it.

He was about to run when they turned onto the wide boulevard again. On a small rise, across another low stone bridge, stood a magnificent building with wide stone steps. Six tall columns across the front of the building, and more columns down each side, supported a flat roof. An imposing dome was visible behind the roof. Again, reminding Adam of structures he'd seen when he'd visited Rome, and leaving no doubt this was the temple.

Since he was here, he might as well see what this Noor person had to say.

Adam followed Orri up the steps and stopped. Behind the center pillars, a life-sized gold statue of six winged horses pulled a chariot. A tall, muscular figure of a man holding a trident, stood inside the chariot. Something about the sculpture took his breath away.

"I've always thought he looks like Noor, but that can't be true because it's a statue of Nethuns," said a female voice.

Adam turned to see a girl with long red hair and large blue eyes. She looked like she was about the same age as him.

She frowned. "Who are you?"

Many people on the street seemed to know his name, so why didn't this girl. "You don't know who I am?"

The girl chewed the corner of her lip for a moment before a look of recognition came over her face. "You're...Adam of Earth." Her eyes fixed on his. "Where did you come from? When did you get here? Have you seen Noor and the council?" The questions came out in one long stream of words running into each other.

Adam opened his mouth to speak, but the girl interrupted.

"Sorry, I know I shouldn't ask so many questions." She thrust out her hand. "I'm Tya."

Orri appeared from behind the statue and glared at the girl. "I'm taking him to the council, and I don't need your help."

"Hold on." Tya put her hands on her hips. "I'm part of this too. Have you asked him why he's here now?"

"No," Orri snapped. "We don't need him. We already have three. You, me and Caileen."

Adam wondered what this Caileen person had to do with him, and then Orri's words sank in. "If you don't need me, then why didn't you tell me how to get home?"

"Because." Orri yanked Adam's sleeve. "Noor will explain everything."

"He's right." Tya shook her head as if she hated to admit what Orri said was true. "We have to talk to Noor."

Adam hoped he'd get some answers from this Noor person. The three of them entered the temple. Crossing an echoing marble space behind the statue, they stopped in the arched doorway of a large room. The ceiling soared above them. Ribs of stone radiated from a round opening in the roof and flowed in graceful curves down to the floor. Light poured into the room from the opening, illuminating several men and women wearing white robes. They sat on low, backless chairs around a circular marble table, and they were arguing.

Chapter Three

"Excuse me," **Orri** said in a loud voice.

Everyone stopped talking and turned to stare at them. Mouths dropped and brows furrowed.

Why were they looking at him like that? Adam tried to swallow the big lump forming in his throat. He should have gone back to the gate.

A tall man, with long snow-white hair melting into his white tunic, rose to his feet. His sculptured face reminded Adam of a comic book superhero, except for the wrinkles showing his great age. Like the face of the man in the golden statue, only older. Adam gazed up into the green eyes that were the same colour as his own and he wanted to trust this man who appeared to be, well, an ancient superman.

"Adam, Son of Earth," the man murmured.

The eyes of the others at the table widened. Some stared at him, some stared at the old man, and several muttered under their breath.

"I am Noor."

This was too creepy. "Why does everyone know my name?" Adam blurted.

Noor studied him for a long moment, his lips curved up softening his face. "Your arrival has been prophesied," he said.

A chill ran down Adam's neck. "Where...?" his throat closed on the words.

"You are in the city of Atlantis," Noor answered.

Atlantis? Adam would have laughed if he hadn't been in shock.

"I can see you do not believe me. Many on Earth think our city was destroyed a long time ago." The old man's words were soothing. "They are wrong. Atlantis has existed for thousands of years."

"Adam claims he came through the gate." Orri's mouth twisted in disbelief.

A heavy silence fell as Noor raised his eyebrows. "No one has entered through the gate in five hundred years."

"I don't really know how I got here. All I know is I was swimming, and I followed a little fish. He led me to the gate, and when my hand touched the bars of the gate, I ended up here." Adam's heart thundered in his chest, making it difficult for him to breathe.

All eyes focused once again on him. Some people smiled at him, a couple seemed concerned, and one man looked at him like he was a bug under a microscope. A bug the man wanted to squash.

Adam couldn't speak. How had he ended up so far from home by touching a dumb underwater gate?

His dad would be mad.

And his mom...

"This must be very confusing for you."

This was a dream. It couldn't be real.

Noor pulled a chair out. "Sit, and I will explain."

Adam slumped onto the seat.

"Orri. Tya." Noor waved at them. "Come in, you two. You are a part of this as well."

Tya perched on a chair beside Adam. She glanced at him with a small smile playing at the corners of her mouth like she was glad he was here. Without saying a word, Tya turned toward Noor. Orri reluctantly took a seat beside the girl. Staring across the table, he ignored the other two.

Noor gracefully settled himself next to Adam. He looked at the people seated around the circular table and smiled "Now that everyone is here, I can explain what is happening."

Adam noticed that all the chairs around the table were filled.

"The gate you came through is a dimensional portal," Noor

said as if he spoke about something ordinary.

"I touched the gate accidentally," Adam protested. "I didn't mean to go through it."

"You left Earth," Noor continued as if he hadn't heard Adam. "And entered the thirteenth dimension, where Atlantis exists. That is why you can see the ocean through the gate but can't get to it."

Adam tried to swallow. "The thirteenth...what?"

"The thirteenth dimension is a place, or perhaps I should call it a version of a place," said Noor. "It can be explained by theories your scientists would call quantum physics."

The thirteenth dimension. Quantum physics. None of this made sense. His eyes desperately scanned the room. He just wanted to go home. He had to go home.

Noor touched his shoulder, drawing Adam's attention back. "You are here because Atlantis needs your help."

Help? Adam jumped to his feet. No! He couldn't help anyone. He was the one who needed help. "But I know nothing about Atlantis." Adam swallowed hard. "Please, tell me how to get home before my parents find out I'm missing."

"Do not worry about your family," Noor said in a gentle voice. "They do not know you have left Earth. Atlantis is in a different dimension, time spent here is not noticed on Earth. There is more." Noor gazed into Adam's eyes. "Once you came through the gate, many things changed, including you."

"This is crazy!" Adam backed away from the table, his heart pounding. "What are you talking about? I haven't changed! I can't help you!"

"You could get through the gate because you can connect with the energy in the universe." Noor rose slowly to his feet and took a step toward Adam. "And because of that ability, you are special. You *can* help Atlantis. After you have done what you came here to do, you will be able to go home."

"You're keeping me here?" he cried, his voice echoing on the curved marble ceiling.

"No, Adam," said Tya. "No one is keeping you here. There simply isn't any way out." She glanced hesitantly at Noor. "Until the prophecy is fulfilled."

Noor pressed his lips together and nodded.

Adam's shoulders drooped. "Everything would be so much easier if I didn't feel vibrations from the earth. Why can't I just be normal?"

"Ah, I see." Noor said in a soothing undertone. "You think you are not normal and that is bad."

It *was* bad. He had never explained his weird feelings to his parents, and he couldn't tell his friends because they would think he was creepy. No one would want to be around him, he'd be picked on, and his life would be a nightmare.

Noor led him back to his seat. "You could think of it as being extraordinary instead. Personally, I think being extraordinary is a good thing." Noor smiled. "Take me, for example..."

A small, bald man loudly cleared his throat.

"Maybe that should be a story for another day." Noor nodded at the bald man before he turned his gaze back to Adam. "You do not realize how unique you are. With the talent you have, you are destined to do amazing things."

Adam shook his head. "You don't understand. I don't have talent."

"I am not explaining this very well." Noor rubbed his chin. "Your being here is a good thing, both for you and for Atlantis."

The light from the opening overhead disappeared, and crystals inset in the walls glowed. Exhaustion from all that had happened weighed on Adam's shoulders.

"I can see you are tired and hungry," said Noor. "Have something to eat. I find things always seem much better on a full stomach." Noor placed a small bowl in front of him, containing what appeared to be three white peas.

That wouldn't fill him up.

"This is pancha. We eat this in Atlantis." Tya pushed the bowl closer to him. "Try one. It's really good."

Adam picked a pea up and put it on his tongue. He closed his mouth, unsure of what might happen. The hard seed dissolved, and his mouth filled with the flavors of his favorite supper, his mother's lasagna. The tastes and smells of the food filled his senses. Like a warm hug from his mom, it comforted him. "Wow, this is awesome!"

Reaching into the bowl for another helping of lasagna he glanced at Tya. Not wanting to be rude, Adam nudged the bowl toward her. She smiled and shook her head. When he popped the pancha into his mouth, he forgot all about Tya. This time, to his surprise, he tasted his favorite dessert, an ice cream sundae with caramel sauce. The seed disappeared on his tongue. Adam sighed and pushed the bowl away, too full to take another bite.

"A lot has happened, and you will need time to adjust." Noor put a hand on Adam's shoulder and gave it a squeeze. "Everything will be as it should."

The warmth from Noor's hand flowed into Adam's body, and he looked up into the old man's kind eyes. He sure hoped Noor was right.

Noor smiled. "Rest for a little while and we will talk later." He turned to Orri. "Orri, take Adam to your room."

A flash of anger swept over Orri's face, but he recovered with a swift smile that failed to reach his eyes. "Yes, sir."

Orri exited the chamber and Adam stumbled behind him, not sure how to protest that he couldn't stay here overnight. Looking at Orri's rigid shoulders, he doubted that he could say anything to the other boy that would make any difference.

They walked down a wide, grey stone hallway lit by gleaming crystals ensconced on the walls. The curved, painted ceiling high above their heads looked like a blue sky with fluffy white clouds. After turning a corner into narrower hallway, Orri stopped. He swiveled around and grabbed two fistfuls of Adam's tunic, shoving him up against the wall.

"Hey, let me go!" Adam struggled to get his feet back on the floor.

"Listen to me," growled Orri, his face close to Adam's, "you are not going to replace Caileen, no matter what Noor says." His lip curled. "I will be the one to lead the trio that saves Atlantis, and I don't need you screwing things up."

"Hey! I tried to leave, remember?"

"Find a way out of here as soon as you can, or you'll be sorry."

Orri dropped him, and stalked away to the next corner. "Are you coming?" he asked in a calm voice showing no trace of the anger there a minute ago.

Adam smoothed his rumpled tunic with shaking hands. Orri was crazy.

"Well?"

Adam gritted his teeth. He had no choice. He had to follow Orri because he didn't know where else to go. "I guess so." He trailed after Orri as he walked down several more hallways. One thought repeated in his brain...I have to get out of here.

Entering a room with two beds, Orri took a crystal from a niche in the wall. He stared at it until it glowed, then placed it on a table between the beds. He cleared a pile of clothes off one bed and threw them in the corner, then indicated Adam should take that bed.

Great. He got to share a room with Orri and his stinky clothes. He flopped down and turned to the wall.

The blankets on the other bed rustled as Orri lay down.

Adam tried to get comfortable, kicking off his sandals and pulling the covers over himself. What was he doing here? He missed his family. A heavy weight pressed on his chest. Now he wished he had helped his sisters clean up. He loved his adoptive family. He had lived with them for as long as he could remember.

Was everything all his fault? Would he be here if his family had understood him better?

He didn't know.

The questions slipped out of his mind and Noor's voice played in his head. "Rest for a little while..."

Chapter Four

Noor watched the boys leave. And so it begins, he thought.

He inhaled deeply, and the tight band of fear around his chest eased. Maybe they could save Atlantis.

"Tya, get some rest too." Noor touched her shoulder. "I will send someone for you when it is light again."

Tya nodded and left the council chamber, closing the door behind her.

Noor knew the studious young girl could help Adam adapt to Atlantis.

He turned to the rest of the council seated around the circular table. Some gazed at the door, as if their thoughts were on the young people. Others seemed lost in their own musings. Some shook their heads and stared at him.

Noor summed up what they were all thinking. "As you all know, the black cloud appeared over the ocean a few days ago, and it has moved closer to Atlantis. Adam's appearance means we cannot ignore it anymore."

"Noor, what have you done?" Cavan questioned him with narrowed eyes.

"I did nothing." Cavan, Noor's main opponent on council, thought he was trying to stop the special training Cavan's daughter, Caileen, was receiving.

"Then how did the boy get here?"

Several around the table murmured to one another.

"I did not bring him here! This is the prophecy at work. Because the black cloud is near, it tells us dark energy has found a way into Atlantis. The cloud will destroy our home if we do not do something about it."

"How do you know that?" Thuan cried. "It might not get strong enough to hurt us!"

"We cannot stop what has been started," replied Noor. How could Thuan still believe that if they didn't fight the black cloud, it wouldn't grow big enough to harm them?

"Maybe we can!" Vannen yelled. "Maybe we should send the new boy away!" Vannen often sided with Thuan, and Noor knew it was because he feared change, too.

Everyone shouted their conflicting opinions at once. The voices got louder and sharper, until they sounded like a squawking murder of crows.

"We have no choice." Raine pounded his fist on the table, his bald head flushed. "The boy is here now, he must be trained!"

"Stop!" Alima scrambled onto her chair to make her tiny frame commanding.

The room fell silent.

"What is happening to us?" she demanded. After a deep breath, she continued in a quieter voice. "This is not how the council makes decisions. We are a democracy. We debate with respect and we follow the prophecies." She shook her head and stepped down. "Dark energy must be affecting us, too."

No one said anything. Noor took a seat before continuing. "Alima is right. Let us begin again."

"The council must decide whether or not to train Adam and the others," said Raine in a calmer voice even though a frown remained on his face.

Vannen shook his head, his long red hair swaying back and forth. "None of them should be trained. They are too young."

"Are we sure he is Son of Earth?" Thuan crossed his arms over his large chest.

"He came through the gate." Noor leaned forward on his elbows. "When you put that together with the timing of his arrival, his name, and the colour of his eyes, could there be any doubt he is Son of Earth?" He looked at each person seated around the table.

"Do not forget," Cavan scowled at Noor, "my daughter,

Caileen, can be trained instead of him."

"Our destiny is to keep Atlantis free of dark energy," Rute said in her quiet, confident way. "We cannot ignore the prophecy." She turned to Cavan. "Caileen is like a daughter to me, but her mixed heritage is a problem. Because she draws her energies from both Earth and Sky, it would be difficult for her to be an energy caster. Now that the boy is here, we must train him instead."

"Rute is correct. What is happening here is bigger than all of us," said Noor. "And destiny overrules choice. We need thirteen people with special energy skills to be able to move Atlantis to safety. The question we must decide is: do we train Adam, Orri and Tya? "

The light from the crystals softened and a hush embraced the room. Noor and the council members settled on their cushions. Noor turned to his right. "I call the vote."

Raine's blue crystal pendant lit up. Alima nodded and her pink pendant glowed, too. Cavan shook his head and his pendant remained dark. Going around the circle, some pendants lit up, and some didn't.

"The vote is cast. Adam of Earth will be trained with Orri of Sky and Tya of Sea," announced Noor. "Now we have to get the new boy to agree to the training."

Although he had denied Cavan's accusation, Noor wondered if Adam arriving in Atlantis did have something to do with him.

Chapter Five

Adam dreamed that he watched from some high point, as enormous black clouds cracking with thunder obliterated the blue sky. Chunks of molten lava spewed from the mouth of a volcano, raining fire on the island of Atlantis. Citizens screamed in the city's streets, their clothes on fire, their homes collapsing. The outer ring of the city rolled and pitched, demolishing everything sitting on its writhing surface. A tsunami, over a hundred feet high, swept toward the city, reaching out to destroy everything in its path.

Then, Adam sat in the temple with twelve others gathered in a circle around the stone table. They held hands, and in his dream, they seemed oblivious to the horror unfolding around them. An electric pulse of energy surged into his hands from the people on either side of him.

The city shimmered and disappeared as the huge wave crashed over the island.

Adam's whole body shook violently. His eyes sprang open, and he scrambled to sit up. Was the room shaking? No, but the dream still echoed through his body. Dazed, he looked around the chamber. "Where am I?"

"We're not going to go through that again, are we?" Orri righted the crystal which had toppled over.

Orri wore a scowl on his face and Adam knew exactly where he was. A pang of homesickness hit him. "What time is it?"

"It's later than you think." Orri shoved a pancha into his hand. "Now get up. Noor sent me to wake you, everyone is waiting for you."

"What does that mean, can't you just tell me it's 9 o'clock if that's what time it is?" Adam ate the tiny piece of food and was rewarded with crisp cereal and milk.

"What's 9 o'clock? Time is relative. It is day, or it is night and time to rest. We don't measure it. What do they teach you on Earth? That is where you are from, isn't it?" Orri stepped toward the door.

Time is relative? Really? He frowned at Orri, trying his best to straighten his wrinkled clothes. "Why do you have to be so difficult? All I did was ask you what time it was."

"Why do you have to be so stupid? Why can't you get it through your head, it doesn't work like that here," replied Orri, as he walked out of the room.

Adam jumped up and ran after him. The last thing he wanted to do was to follow Orri anywhere, but he had no way to get to the council chambers without him.

Noor stood and smiled when Orri and Adam entered the central chamber. A golden light infused the room from above. Had any of them slept, Adam wondered. Yes, several wore clean clothes, and they appeared fresh and rested, if still worried. Noor motioned for them to take their seats and lowered himself onto a chair. "Please sit. We need to talk."

Adam dropped onto an empty chair between Tya and Orri. Tya smiled at him, like she had the day before. Adam was glad she was there.

"You must excuse my manners," Noor said. "I did not introduce you to the council yesterday. This is Raine." Noor gestured toward a short man with bright blue eyes. He was bald and had a round face with large ears sticking straight out on each side, giving him a gnome-like look. "He is our resident scientist."

The man placed his hands together in front of his chest and bowed his head.

Adam, unsure what to do, bowed his head in response.

"And Alima is our healer."

The tiny woman had a long grey braid over one shoulder. She had nearly as many wrinkles as Noor, but when she smiled, her face became almost youthful. She reminded Adam of his grandmother, and a wave of loneliness washed over him.

"Cavan is our librarian," Noor continued. The man had a narrow face, and a mouth set in a thin line. This was the man that had looked at Adam like he was a bug yesterday, and he was doing it again.

The floor shivered, and Adam clutched at the edge of the table. The members of the council cast worried glances at one another.

"That is the second tremor in four days," Raine muttered. It was quiet enough that Adam was pretty sure only Noor was supposed to hear it. Noor continued as if neither the tremor nor the comment had affected him.

Noor introduced the rest of the council, but after the tremor, Adam couldn't concentrate. He could still feel Cavan's eyes boring into him. Names and faces blurred together...Vannen, Thuan, Rute and several other names he couldn't remember.

Noor cleared his throat. "We have much to discuss if you are going to be prepared to help us. A long time ago, when Atlantis existed on Earth, the island was destroyed."

"By a tsunami," Adam whispered, the terror of his dream clear in his mind.

"Yes." Noor leaned forward. "How did you know?"

Adam blinked away the vision. "I had a dream. It felt...I don't know, like I was really there."

"That is not possible!" Cavan jumped to his feet. "He is lying. Someone must have told him."

Adam flinched at Cavan's outburst.

"He is telling the truth." Noor spoke in a firm voice, permitting no arguments. "No one could have told him. Tell us the rest of your dream."

Adam told them about the council and the shimmering city just before the tsunami hit, just has he'd seen it in his dream.

Noor smiled, "The dream channeling is another confirmation of his connection to Atlantis."

"What is dream channeling?" asked Adam.

"Important details about the past or the future come to you

when your mind is open, like when you are asleep. It is a skill only a few have." Noor smiled at Alima before returning his gaze to Adam. "And it is a powerful tool once you learn how to use it."

"I don't understand why this is happening to me." Adam's stomach tightened.

"Because of the prophecy. You are needed here." Noor held up his hand to stop Adam from speaking. "When the tsunami you dreamed about annihilated the island of Atlantis, the city itself was not destroyed because the council could save it. It takes thirteen of us to move the city. Over the centuries, Atlantis has moved several times. Some of those moves happened when the city still existed on Earth."

Adam stared at him. So many questions filled his head but one stood out—how could they move a city?

The floor shivered again, stronger this time. Adam shot a glance at Tya. She shrugged, but her face paled.

"The people on Earth are finding a few of those places," said Noor. The corner of Noor's mouth lifted briefly as if he was amused by the discoveries, but just as quickly his tone became solemn again. "Today, we cannot move Atlantis to safety because there are only ten of us." Noor gestured to include the rest of the council.

A deep rumbling sound erupted from beneath the floor, building to a deafening roar.

"Take cover," bellowed Noor. The floor shuddered and everyone scrambled to get under the table.

Adam gripped the table, bewildered.

"Adam," Noor reached out to him.

He peeled the fingers of one hand away from the table and stretched toward Noor. The floor pitched and he tumbled off his seat, hitting his head. His vision blurred with dancing stars.

His arm was being pulled out of its socket as his back scraped across the stone surface. A thundering crash reverberated beside him, sending another stabbing pain through his head.

Then all became still. For how long he couldn't tell.

"Adam, can you hear me?"

Pain pounded in Adam's head. He sat up carefully and

squinted at Noor.

They were all crouched under the council table. Thankfully, the floor had stopped moving. "What happened?" He put his hand to his head.

"We had a tremor. Other than you, no one got hurt." Noor glanced over his shoulder at the others. "I think it is safe for everyone to come out now."

Noor helped Adam out from under the table. A large chunk of stone from the roof had flattened the chair where he had been sitting a few moments before.

"We were fortunate." Noor squeezed his shoulder. "It could have been worse."

Adam's pulse quickened.

"Alima, would you have a look at Adam's head?" Noor asked.

Alima reached up to put her hands on the back of his head. To Adam's surprise, she was much shorter than he was. Her hands were warm, and the pounding in his head stopped as soon as she touched him. She smiled up at him and her eyes twinkled. "You will live."

"I hope so."

"The tremors are occurring more often," said Alima. "but it is our job to protect you." She patted his arm.

Again, she reminded him of his grandmother. Thinking of his grandmother comforted him, but wow, he missed her. Somehow, he had to find a way to get home.

"This is another confirmation. Dark energy is threatening Atlantis." Noor looked at Adam. "And your help is needed so we can save our city."

"But, I already told you, I don't know how," said Adam.

"We will train you, so you can learn to use your talent." Noor's even voice made the statement as if it was a fact.

"I can't stay here for training." Noor didn't get it. "I have to get home."

"We don't need him." Orri leapt to his feet. "I can do this." Orri gazed down at Tya and his cheeks flushed. "*We* can do this. Me, Tya and Caileen."

Noor scowled at Orri. "We have already discussed this. The

prophecy says, 'One from the sky and one from the sea, and one from the earth will set us free.'"

"Adam is from Earth," added Alima as she gazed at Orri. "That is why it has to be him and not Caileen."

Orri slouched on his seat, crossed his arms and stared at Adam.

Adam turned toward Noor to avoid Orri's eyes. "What is this prophecy you keep talking about?"

"The prophecy says three special people will be added to the ten council members," Noor said, "and then we will be able to save Atlantis. We think the three are you, Tya and Orri."

"Why me?" Adam looked wildly around the room. "What about this Caileen person Orri and Cavan talked about?"

"No." Noor's eyes pinned him to the floor. "It has to be you. You are the one from the People of the Earth."

"Don't I get a choice? I mean, shouldn't I get some sort of say in this? You brought me here and tell me that I must help you because it is prophesied. I don't know what that means. All I want to do is go home. And if none of you will help me, then I will just have to figure out how to do that on my own."

"Yeah, shaking the gate really worked, didn't it?" Orri smirked.

Adam spun around, but Tya spoke before he could, "Quit being such a bully, Orri." She glared at him.

"Aren't you listening? He wants to go home," said Orri.

"Ignore him." Tya came over to Adam and spoke in a quiet voice so the others couldn't hear. "Adam, we need you."

The colour of her eyes reminded him of a faded pair of blue jeans. No girl had ever looked at him like that. He felt hot and self-conscious, but he liked it.

"I understand wanting to go home, but we need you, and you have to learn about your energy first." Tya gave him the look again. "I think that if you look deep in your heart, you know you're supposed to be here. What you feel, the homesickness, isn't going away."

How could she be so sure of herself?

"Besides, you won't be missed on Earth. Time is different

here. They won't even know you're gone. And we need you here," Tya said.

"I don't know. Everyone keeps telling me what to do," Adam stuttered, trying to swallow the lump in his throat. "I feel trapped..."

"And you're scared," added Tya.

Adam stared at his feet to avoid her gaze. Yes, he was scared.

"I would be too," she said gently. "Listen. Orri and I have started our training, but the council was waiting for a sign that the thirteen was possible. I haven't even got my pendant yet. So, when you start your training, we'd be right there with you. We can do it together. I can help you if you want me to."

Maybe she could help. Maybe she could be his friend. She said his parents wouldn't know he was gone. Here was the freedom to be himself. Home was lying, and pretending he was something he wasn't.

Adam turned to look at the council, milling around the jumble of marble that had been their table. Noor watched him. Adam felt the corner of his mouth lift and he spoke to Noor. "I'm still not sure what I'm supposed to do, but...," he shrugged, "maybe..."

Noor smiled. "You are destined to make a difference." He held out an arm, inviting Adam back to the circle. "I know you are confused, but we are all here to help. You are not alone."

The words 'you are not alone' echoed in Adam's head. Looking up at Noor, something in him shifted. He knew he wouldn't be on his own. He approached the broken table and Noor's outstretched arm. For the first time in his life, someone understood what he felt.

Almost everyone smiled at him. Cavan wasn't smiling, but he didn't have a scowl on his face, either. The only exception was Orri. His brows lowered over fierce eyes, and his mouth set in a thin line.

"You can do this." Noor put a comforting arm around his shoulder.

Calmness flowed into Adam and he let out a long, slow breath. With the panic and fear withdrawing, the disjointed feelings swirling in his head settled into place like the pieces of a puzzle. Curiosity filled his being. He wasn't a freak in this world. These people felt the same things he did. Even Orri.

Tya's grin widened as she joined the group.

Then he fixed his eyes on Orri. You can't stop me, he thought. In a voice steadier than he felt he said, "I'll do the training."

Chapter Six

"Orri, Adam and Tya will receive their pendants and complete their training," announced Noor. "We will have the pendant ceremony at the Plaza of Athena. Cavan, bring the bowl and meet us there."

Cavan nodded and slipped out of the room.

"What's happening?" Adam whispered to Tya.

Tya's eyes filled with excitement. "Oh, Adam! We are going to be given pendants to use when we work with energy," she squealed in a barely contained whisper. "It is an important step in our training."

"Everyone, follow me," said Noor, before Adam could ask any more questions.

Adam didn't know if he would ever understand what happened in this place. Maybe he shouldn't have agreed so easily.

Noor led the way. Adam and Tya were near the back of the group, with Orri sauntering behind them. The group trailed across a bridge over the canal and down the same main boulevard Orri had used to bring him to the temple. People on the street stopped to ask Noor or the council members for advice, slowing their progress. The greetings were friendly, but uneasy. Earthquakes make everyone edgy.

During one of these stops, Adam glanced up at the sky. It was the same dazzling blue it had been when he arrived, but now he noticed something missing. "Where's the sun?"

Tya tilted her head to one side. "What's a sun?"

Adam stared at her, not sure whether to laugh. "You're kidding, right?"

She squinted at him in confusion.

"It gives you daylight," he said. "And when the sun sets, it's night."

"I don't know what you're talking about." Tya frowned at him. "Day and night are relative."

Relative. Everyone kept using that word. "What does that mean?"

"We depend on the Time Crystal to turn the light on or off," she shrugged. "And it makes day and night as long or as short as they should be."

"Daylight in Atlantis is controlled by a crystal? There is no sun or moon?"

"This is the thirteenth dimension, remember?" Tya replied as if she lectured to a particularly dense student.

Adam looked up at the sky and shook his head. Tya seemed to know a lot.

"Come on. We're getting left behind." Tya gestured for him to hurry up. They turned left onto a cobbled street that curved to follow the canal. A couple of minutes later they stopped, and Tya stretched her hands out wide. "This is the Plaza of Athena." Her face clearly reflected she thought the plaza was something amazing.

In front of them lay a tiled patio with marble columns on all four sides. Some patio tiles were cracked or missing altogether, and the columns were different heights as if something had randomly broken off the tops. Adam surveyed the plaza. It was just an old ruin. Why did Tya think it was special?

In the center of the patio stood an octagon-shaped, waist-high altar covered with strange carvings that looked like mythical creatures. As the council took their places, people of the city assembled around them, standing at a respectful distance.

Cavan approached the octagonal stone with a golden bowl filled with dozens of coloured, marble-sized stones. He set the bowl on top of the altar and stared at Adam. The corners of his mouth turned up as if he was trying to smile, but his cheeks didn't move and his eyes weren't smiling.

A shiver ran up Adam's back.

Noor gestured for Adam to stand beside him. "This must seem very strange, but you will understand more as you receive your training." Then, louder, "It is time to pick your pendant. Put your hand into the bowl."

Adam shoved his hand into the almost full bowl, and three of the small stones glowed. He yanked his hand back. The stones went dark and the crowd gasped. Everyone spoke at once.

"I've never seen that before!"

"What kind of trickery is this?"

"How did he do that?" shouted Orri.

"Silence!" Noor turned to Adam and in a quieter voice he said, "Put your hand in the bowl again."

"Did I do something wrong?" A swarm of butterflies fluttered in Adam's stomach.

"No. It is all right," said Noor. "Go ahead. Try again."

In the hush, Adam cautiously slid his fingers back into the bowl. The same three stones lit up again.

Noor picked the stones up and set them down beside the bowl.

Looking closely at them, Adam saw they were not stones at all. They were small crystals, each carved in the shape of a skull. An emerald green one, a turquoise one, and a clear one. Cool.

"Pick one up," directed Noor.

Not knowing why, Adam felt pulled toward the clear skull. He reached for it but couldn't make his hand touch it. Something held him back. Now the green skull caught his attention. Which one should he pick?

Closing his eyes, Adam grabbed a skull. He opened his eyes and saw the green skull glowing brightly in his hand.

You chose correctly, a strange whispery voice told him.

Adam looked around not sure where the voice came from.

Down here.

Adam felt a strong vibration flow into his body from the tiny skull. He closed his hand around the skull. This feeling he recognized.

"Well, it seems to be the one," said Noor.

"Yes, that's what it told me." Adam opened his hand.

"Your energy is strong when you feel it so easily." Noor smiled.

"No, the skull spoke to me."

Again, the throng talked all at once. Noor ignored them. "Are you sure it actually spoke?"

"Yes. Isn't it supposed to?"

"There are many kinds of skulls and some talk when they are touched. But skull pendants, like the one you hold, cannot be heard by most people." Noor rubbed his chin. "This green skull is definitely yours, but what to do with the other two skulls? To have more than one skull light up is unusual."

Set me down, the low voice of the green skull commanded Adam. *Pick up the other two skulls and you will know what to do with them.* Somehow, he knew that he needed to obey the skull's directions without question.

You should have picked me, the clear skull growled, making Adam's skin crawl. *You don't know how powerful we could have been. Give me to the other boy instead.*

Adam held the clear skull out toward Orri and it flickered. The gathering rumbled with mutterings.

Orri stepped back and scowled at Noor. "Why should he get to choose my skull?"

"Sometimes we must trust the universe. You could not pick a skull before, and Adam has chosen three skulls. Take the skull."

Orri snatched it from Adam's hand. The skull became brighter when Orri touched it.

Adam turned toward Tya and the remaining skull glowed. When he placed the stone in her hand, her face split with a grin.

"Thank you," she said.

Collecting the skulls from the children, Noor closed his hand around the three stones. A moment later he opened his hand, and somehow each little skull hung from a chain. "Here are your pendants."

Noor gave Adam and Tya their skull pendants, and the people cheered. Adam placed his around his neck, self-conscious at the attention.

Orri grabbed his pendant from Noor's outstretched hand.

Adam shook his head. Orri was such a pain.

Noor stood before the three children. "Everything is energy. Only a few of us can connect with it and change it. You will learn how to join with energy, to channel energy using your pendant, and to change energy." A thoughtful look passed across Noor's face. "By necessity, your training must be brief. This will make it difficult, it will test you, but the dangers we all face are real, and we have no time to lose."

Adam's shoulders slumped. Now, it sounded like he might not live to get home. A twinge of homesickness stabbed him. He swallowed hard against the lump in his throat.

Noor changed his tone. "Not to worry. You have been chosen because you are courageous and you will be able to do what needs to be done. Your training starts now."

Again, the crowd cheered.

Chapter Seven

James, Chief Archaeologist at the Drumdyre archeological site in northern Scotland, leaned into the wind that blew incessantly at the site, rain or shine. His team had almost finished the excavations, and the 5000-year-old Scottish settlement had revealed some amazing information.

He entered his makeshift office and pushed the door closed against the gale. James turned to see Adrian Zador sitting behind his desk.

"Adrian," James acknowledged the stylishly dressed man wearing a well-tailored business suit, an impeccably pressed shirt, and perfectly shined shoes. With not a hair out of place, his appearance suited a fancy New York office rather than this cramped, disorganized workspace.

Zador leaned back in James' chair, his body relaxed as he gazed at the archeologist on the other side of the desk. "I know it's here," he said.

"The skull isn't here." James moved to the tiny sideboard and plugged in the coffeemaker. "Drumdyre has nothing to do with Atlantis."

"Oh, but it does."

James frowned. He resented having to report to this man, who provided the much needed, though not exactly legal, financing for the excavation. But what really made the chief archaeologist edgy, was being told what artifacts he should find. A crystal skull wouldn't be at a 5000-year-old Neolithic site. Especially not one on an island off the northern coast of Scotland. "We've almost finished the dig. There's no evidence what you are seeking is here." James pretended to look for a cup and spoon so he wouldn't have to look at the man. "Why do you think we will find it?"

"A powerful man told me. He wouldn't lie to me." Zador stood up and moved around the desk to stand in front of James. He put a hand on the archeologist's wrist to command his attention.

James gazed into the soulless eyes of the man leaning toward him, and his breath caught in his throat.

"Find the skull. It will not turn out well if you disappoint me." Zador left the office.

The door banged in the wind behind him.

Chapter Eight

When they entered the third hallway since following Raine into the building, Adam realized the temple was much larger on the inside than it appeared from the outside. Several doors lined each side of this corridor, and no two were alike. Raine stopped and opened a door made of some kind of metal. The door was thick and looked like it could withstand a major explosion, or perhaps an earthquake. Raine preceded the three of them into a room that looked like the lab of a mad scientist.

Chunks of crystal on the ceiling and walls lit the room in a rainbow of colours. Drawings of beings with misshapen skulls and orb-like eyes were pinned on the wall, a few human-sized crystal skulls lay scattered about on tables and shelves, and several strange metal contraptions hung from the ceiling. Jars filled with bizarre objects floating in murky liquids sat on shelves. His nose wrinkled at the moldy smell, and his head filled with ideas of how they ended up in there. A shiver ran down Adam's spine, wondering what Raine used the devices for. Maybe Raine secretly killed the subjects of his experiments to harvest their parts. If something died in here, no one would ever find it.

"Better keep up, Earth Boy," Orri whispered, turning his head. Then as if reading his mind, "or you'll end up in a jar."

Adam gritted his teeth so he wouldn't react to the older boy's slight.

Raine took a winding path through the crowded room, stopping short when he reached an open space at the back. The trio slid into each other, and Orri's elbow dug into Adam's ribs. Adam would not let the bully push him around. His knuckles connected with Orri's lower back.

Orri swiveled around with his fists raised.

"Stop that!" scolded Raine preventing Orri from punching Adam. "Sit down!"

Orri started it, thought Adam, as he sat on the other side of Tya, away from the older boy.

In contrast to Noor's graceful presence, Raine's energy exuded so vigorously it was easy to ignore his small stature. When Raine focused his intense eyes on him, Adam forgot there was anyone else in the room.

"It is my job to teach you how to change energy," said Raine. "Your training will start at the beginning."

Orri groaned. "This is your fault, Earth boy."

"I see you believe you are smarter than that." Raine lowered his eyebrows and fixed his gaze on Orri. "You still have much to learn, and Tya can use the review. Instead of being angry and closing your mind, open it. You may be amazed at what you will discover."

Orri rolled his eyes when Raine turned away.

Adam concentrated on Raine, ignoring the older boy.

"You have all shown that you have the ability to draw energy from the world around you like a tree draws water from the soil," said Raine. "For you, it is as natural as breathing. That is why you are here."

Natural. Like breathing. Adam couldn't believe what he was hearing. After spending most of his life not being understood he had stumbled on an entire world of people who knew what he felt, because they felt it, too. He thought back to a couple of weeks ago, walking home from school. He'd seen a small rock lying in the gutter. Just a stone, nothing special about its smooth grey surface, but it beckoned to Adam. He reached down and picked it up. When he did, a zap surged up his arm and into his head—fierce and immediate. It hadn't seemed natural, but maybe in this world, it could be.

Raine's voice brought Adam back to reality. "Energy and matter are the same thing. We simply rearrange atoms using our energy."

Out of the corner of his eye, Adam saw a smile skitter across Tya's mouth.

"You can use thought to do this. Training will teach you how, and practice will make you stronger."

Wow! Change objects with thought? "How can we do that?" asked Adam.

"If you listen, I will tell you. But if you interrupt me, we will never get there." Raine narrowed his eyes at Adam, and Orri chuckled.

Okay, okay, he'd shut up.

Raine cleared his throat. "Atlantis is made up of three types of people: People of the Sky, Earth and Sea. Each of you comes from a different people. It is easy to tell who comes from which ancestry by their eye colour. Green for Earth, grey for Sky and blue for Sea."

That was where the Son of Earth came from. But how...? Adam opened his mouth to ask the question, Raine's eyebrows lowered, and Adam pinched his lips together. Right, no questions. School in Atlantis was just like school at home.

"The people you come from also determines the way you feel energy, and how you will work with it." Raine's eyes swept over the three seated in front of him. "Any place where air, land and water connect, like on a beach, is where all three of you feel the strongest connection with your energy. That is because it is a place where the elements join and work well together."

It explained the way Adam felt on the beach. Adam watched Orri's normally cool grey eyes darken to the colour of a storm cloud as he stared at him. That Sky would not work well with this Earth.

"Although it is easier to use your skull pendant to work with energy," Raine continued. "We will start your energy practice without using a pendant. Orri and Tya have both done this."

"Earth Boy needs it to be easier," whispered Orri.

Don't say anything. Don't say anything. Adam clenched his fists.

Again, Raine showed his displeasure, this time at Orri.

Adam smiled, and Orri dropped his eyes to avoid Raine's

glare.

"All right then, let us begin. Stand up," commanded Raine. "Imagine yourself touching your element."

Adam stood. Watch me, Sky Boy. I'm as good as you. He visualized standing on the beach, and the familiar sensation shimmered in the soles of his feet.

"Feel the energy!"

Adam's feet rooted into the floor. A heavy pleasant feeling filled his belly as if something great was about to happen. The familiar vibration moved in waves up his body, and into his head. The awareness cocooned him and a warm breeze caressed his face.

Three tennis ball-sized white lights appeared above them, bouncing wildly around the ceiling.

"Focus energy on one of the lights and make it stop," said Raine.

Orri easily controlled a light.

Concentrating on another light, Adam tried to halt it. The bouncing light zipped from one corner to another. His eyes darted back and forth, unable to keep up with its crazy path.

"Control your light. Do not let it control you," admonished Raine.

"How?"

"Think! What do you want the light to do?"

All the thoughts in Adam's brain screamed stop! The light froze in place.

This is so cool! Adam grinned and glanced at Raine. His light flew madly around the room again.

"If your mind wanders, you cannot do this," Raine said in a stern voice.

Adam immobilized the light for a second time. It wiggled, trying to break free, but Adam kept it in one place. He did it!

Raine didn't notice him because Tya now had his attention. She couldn't seem to figure out how to direct her light and kept losing control.

"Tya, I know you can do this." Raine shook his head. "You have done it before. You need to concentrate."

"It's too hard. I can't do it," Tya said between clenched teeth.

"Teacher's pet can't tell left from right." Orri laughed.

"One more comment like that and you will be asked to leave the room." Raine glared at Orri.

"Sorry," Orri mumbled. He turned to Tya. "I am sorry, really."

Tya blinked rapidly and nodded.

Adam couldn't believe it. Orri actually apologized?

Running his hands over his bald head, Raine sighed. "Perhaps we should try something else. Let us work on channeling your energy through the pendant. On your pendant, you can see a silver piece shaped like a hand at the top of the skull. It acts as an amplifier to channel your energy into the skull pendant, and strengthen it."

With Raine's guidance, Adam focused all the feelings swirling through his body into the small skull resting on his chest. The light halted and Adam blinked. It was easy, now.

"Good!" said Raine.

Another light flew by Adam's light. He attempted to stop it too, and both lights flew wildly around the room.

"Pretty dumb, Earth Boy," said Orri.

Adam regained control of his light as Orri's light continued to zoom around the room.

"Worry about your own energy," warned Raine. "There will always be someone better than you are."

The corners of Orri's mouth turned down, and he rubbed his skull pendant.

Tya stood beside Adam, doggedly concentrating on her light as it wiggled in place.

"Well done, Tya," said Raine.

"Teacher's pet," muttered Orri again, but quietly enough that Raine couldn't hear.

Tya's eyes flickered toward Orri, and she lost control of the light again. Squeezing her eyes shut, she shook her head.

"Pay no attention to him," said Raine. "You have almost got it."

He continued to instruct them to perform various moves with their lights: up, down, right, left, in a circle. Adam followed Raine's directions and managed to do most exercises with ease, even with Orri bugging him.

Raine couldn't pay much attention to what the boys were doing, because he had to keep stopping to help Tya. No matter what he told them to do, Tya messed up somehow, by doing it backward, upside down, or so awkwardly, it didn't appear right at all.

As Adam watched her, he realized Orri was correct. She didn't know left from right. What seemed easy for Adam must've been really hard for her.

When Tya noticed both boys were watching her, she gave up altogether. "It's hard enough, but I really can't do this with those two watching me."

"Oh, for Dootz' sake," snapped Raine putting his hands on his hips and frowning at the three of them. "How am I supposed to teach you three anything?"

Although it had been a long day for everyone, Adam had never seen a teacher behave this way. He wondered if it happened often here but seeing the bewildered looks on Orri and Tya's faces, he thought not.

Raine took a deep breath and blew it out noisily. He grabbed a table and moved it in front of them. The table had a small copper-coloured metal contraption on it. It looked like a miniature roller coaster with hills and valleys, backward loops, and spiral drops going in several directions.

"Maybe you can do this," said Raine. He opened his hand, and three marble-sized coloured balls of light appeared on the table. "Now, I want each of you to move a ball through this maze. You will have to work on solving the puzzle and concentrate on using your energy. Adam, you go first."

Adam moved the ball of light with precision through the pathways of the maze. His body became warm from the exertion of concentrating his energy. Enjoying the feeling of accomplishment, he leaned in and moved the light even faster through the maze.

The ball reached the last part of the labyrinth. With his goal in sight, all he had to do was bump the upright section in the track, knocking it into the next series of pieces so they fell in a domino effect. Then, the ball would roll into the cup. Before he had a chance to move it, the small glowing sphere flew out of the maze and jumped wildly about the room. Adam's gaze darted toward the other boy. Orri stared at the light and rubbed his pendant.

"Good try," said Raine. "It is your turn, Orri."

Your turn, Orri, thought Adam. Two could play at this game. Orri didn't even get his light through the first channel, when Adam pushed it back to the starting point. The light twisted in place as the boys battled each other.

"Enough! I cannot teach if you two keep playing around," shouted Raine. "You both need to concentrate!" He pointed to the door, "Leave. I have had enough for today."

Chapter Nine

Noor sat alone in the council chamber. The ceiling and the table
had been repaired, and through the round opening in the center
of the roof, light streamed into the room. The workers taking care
of maintenance were very skilled at using energy to keep the
ancient buildings in good condition.

Raising his face to the ceiling, he let the warmth and light
calm him. He pondered the prophecy, and the signs of its
approach. Too many of the omens were still unclear.

Raine strode in and stood on the other side of the table with
his hands on his hips.

"What happened?"

"The boys are too busy competing with each other to
concentrate. Tya is distracted by their antics and forgetting
everything she has learned about adjusting for her directional
challenges," he fumed. "They will never learn what they need to
learn, in time to help us."

"The prophecy has been set in motion." Noor said. "There is
nothing we can do to stop it now. They will have to learn."

Raine slapped his palms on to the table. "I am a scientist, not
a teacher." He leaned toward Noor. "Why would you think I can
teach those three anything?" Raine shook his head. "I do not have
the patience for it."

"You have the greatest ability to connect with energy, and
that makes you the best person to teach them how to unite with
what they feel," said Noor. "If you can teach them that, Alima and
I will do the rest."

"Flattery will get you nowhere." Raine glowered at him.

Noor said nothing as he waited for his old friend to agree with him.

"Fine." Raine sighed. "I will figure something out and try again tomorrow."

"I know you can do this, my friend." Noor smiled at Raine.

After Raine left, Noor looked up at the opening in the roof again. Drawing a deep breath, he waited for the light to calm his mind. Instead, a sharp pain sliced into his temple. Noor stood up and gripped the edge of the table to stop himself from falling over. A rift had torn through the energy field. He ran from the room.

Chapter Ten

Tya, Orri and Adam walked down the hallway away from Raine's lab, Tya in the lead by half a step.

A wave of tiredness flowed over Adam, like he had just played a soccer game against a tough opponent.

After turning a corner into an empty corridor, Tya swiveled to face the boys. She poked her finger at Orri. "Stop being such a jerk." She turned the accusing finger at Adam. "Stop letting Orri get to you. Ignore him."

Adam crossed his arms over his chest and glared at Tya. "He started it. He's hated me ever since I got here."

"We already have someone, we don't need you. I have been here all my life, I know what I'm doing. I know the stuff you're just learning now, and I'm better than you are."

"Stop it!" Tya moved between the two boys and pushed them apart. "You're both being childish." She glared at Orri. "We have to save Atlantis, and Adam, not Caileen, will be trained with us. Get used to it."

Orri reached up and rubbed his skull pendant. The turbulence in his eyes disappeared and a strange calmness replaced it. He replied in a reasonable voice, "I could do that."

Adam shivered, as if a cold breeze had blown across the back of his neck. Maybe he liked angry Orri better—he was more predictable.

"What Raine taught us today was baby stuff. He's holding us back. We're more advanced than that." Orri turned to Tya. "Why don't we show Adam what he can do with energy?"

"I...I don't think that's a good idea," said Tya.

"Are you scared?" Orri raised an eyebrow at her. He turned to Adam. "Are you?"

Adam was exhausted from all that had happened today but he would not back down. He stood up tall. "I'm not scared. I can do anything you can do."

Tya scowled at Orri. "It's not about being scared."

"So, let's do it," said Orri.

"No." The word sliced through the air. Tya's hand trembled as she pushed a strand of hair behind her ear. "What if something goes wrong? Someone could get hurt...or worse."

"You did this when Caileen trained with us." Orri squinted at her. "What's changed?"

"Adam hasn't done this before. Raine should teach him, not us."

"What do you think Earth Boy? Who are you going to agree with?"

Adam glanced at Tya. All the colour had drained out of her face. She was afraid, but of what?

"What's it gonna be?" Orri nudged Adam's shoulder and grinned at him. "I think you're scared."

No way could he let Orri think that. Adam avoided Tya's gaze and gritted his teeth. "Let's do it."

"You two can do your macho thing, I won't be a part of this. I'm leaving." Tya trudged down the hallway.

Adam watched her walk away. Out of the corner of his eye he could see the smile plastered on Orri's face. His stomach clenched. Adam didn't want to think about what could happen if he was left alone with Orri. "Wait," Adam called just as Tya got to the corner. "Orri's right. The three of us need to practice together."

Tya turned around.

"And I need to learn this stuff so we can do whatever we're supposed to do." Adam hoped he didn't sound too desperate.

Tya didn't move.

"You said you'd help me." The words fell into the space between them. Tya stared at him, but Adam couldn't tell what she felt. Moments ticked by.

"Aww, come on." Orri tilted his head. "Nothing bad will happen."

Tya walked back to them. No one said anything.

"I still think this is a bad idea." She narrowed her eyes at Orri. "I know you'll do this whether I'm here or not, and someone should make sure you two don't kill each other." She sighed. "We need to find a place where we won't be seen."

A satisfied look spread across Orri's face. "Let's go up on the roof. Nobody goes there,"

"The roof?" Adam's voice quivered, and he swallowed hard.

"It's a flat patio in front of the domed roof of the council room," said Tya. "You get a great view of the city from up there."

Easy for her to say. Her world didn't spin when she looked down from high places.

Adam and Tya trailed after Orri as they slinked down the hallways, ending up by the entrance of the temple. Orri crept around the statue of Nethuns, Tya and Adam followed. Orri stared at the blank wall in front of him and then ran his hands over the surface. Smiling, he pressed a marble tile. Adam noticed the tile had a small chip on one corner. When the wall opened, Orri sprinted up the spiraling stone steps without looking back. Glowing crystal sconces emitted a soft light on the treads, guiding Tya and Adam's climb.

When they reached the flat stone surface of the roof, Tya and Orri went to the railing and looked down.

Adam hung back, his gaze fixed on the horizon to avoid the nausea overwhelming him at the thought of peering over the side. At the edge of the city, a dark grey cloud hovered on the horizon distracting him for a moment. "What's that?" he asked.

"That," Tya said, "is the physical form of the dark energy threatening Atlantis. It caused the tremor we felt in the council chamber."

"It looks like a rain cloud." Adam couldn't believe he had agreed to be trained to save Atlantis from a little black cloud. "How could it destroy Atlantis?"

"It doesn't look like much now," said Orri. "but it must be stopped before it grows too big." He shrugged. "I told you, we can do this with Caileen if you don't want to do this."

"Not a chance." Adam lifted his chin. "So, what are you going to show me?"

Tya stepped away from the railing. "Let me do this."

"Of course, you *are* the teacher's pet." Orri held his hands up. "The next step in the training is about shifting energy." Tya launched into her lecture. "It's called molecular transformation."

Molecular what? Adam wished he had listened more in science class.

"The amount of energy in the universe never changes," Tya continued, sounding just like Raine. "We can only shift it. Shifting energy allows us to unlock one reality and form another."

Orri rolled his eyes. "It takes a lot of time in the library to sound like that."

Tya ignored him. She pulled an egg-sized red crystal from her pocket and set it on the patio. "We'll use this for the lesson." She focused on the crystal, narrowing her eyes. It disappeared and reappeared five feet away.

Adam's mouth dropped. Wow, that was so cool. He quickly closed his mouth hoping the others didn't notice his reaction.

Orri snapped his fingers. The crystal disappeared and popped up again in front of Tya, now a light blue colour.

Tya winked at Orri and it vanished again.

The crystal popped in and out of existence so fast, Adam had trouble following it.

As Adam watched, he realized Orri's eyes were bright, and he was actually having fun.

The crystal disappeared and didn't reappear.

Tya chuckled. "Orri, where is it?"

He reached into his pocket and extracted the stone. Bowing he held it out to Tya.

"Awesome!" Adam clapped his hands together. Then, feeling his face burn, he fisted his hands by his side. I'm so nerdy. He turned to Tya, not wanting to see Orri's expression at his geeky reaction. "How did you do that?"

"It's not as hard as it looks. I can show you." Tya took the crystal from Orri and placed it back on the patio. "Start by feeling the form of the object with your mind."

Adam closed his eyes. He saw the image of the red stone in his head and felt the shape as if he touched it with his fingers.

"Let its vibrations echo within you, separate from your own energy rhythms."

The pulse of the crystal travelled into his brain and he could hear the beat like a slow, steady heartbeat.

"Dissolve the object by speeding up its energy vibrations. When the molecular movements are fast enough, it will simply disappear. Look to where you want it to go. Remember the object and the beat in your mind. Slow the molecular energy down to its original speed, bringing it back into existence."

Here was his chance to show Orri what he could do. He concentrated on quickening the crystal's energy. It disappeared.

Adam looked across the patio and a puddle of red, gooey liquid materialized.

"What did I do wrong?" His hands curled into fists again.

"Your vibrations were not quite right," said Tya. "Thinking of the vibrations is like recalling a piece of music. *Feel* the beat. And I forgot to tell you to breathe, too."

Adam gritted his teeth.

"Watch me." Tya took a deep breath and a small frown formed on her face. The crystal goo disappeared. Gazing at the patio, she exhaled, and the crystal appeared solid and whole, exactly as it had been a few moments before.

She made it look so easy. If she could do this so could he. Adam's frustration amplified the energy surging through his body. His temples pounded with the beat of his anger. Forgetting to breathe, he shot an intense look at the crystal. It disappeared with a popping sound. When it reappeared, it wasn't an egg sized crystal at all.

A crystal dagger flew through the air.

Headed at Orri.

Orri raised his hand.

The knife pivoted and shot toward Adam.

Adam ducked.

It clattered to the ground behind him.

"You nearly killed Adam!" Tya yelled.

"He tried to kill me first!" Orri's anger spread, red, up his neck and face.

A cold sweat covered Adam's body. "I wasn't trying to kill you. I made a mistake!" His jaw tightened. "It was your dumb idea to do this."

"Both of you! STOP IT!" Tya's voice cracked, and her hand shook as it covered her mouth.

"What is going on here?" Noor's strong voice carried across the roof.

The three froze. In the quiet, Noor's footsteps clicked on the stone as he strode toward them.

"We umm...were helping Adam." Tya's voice was so low, Adam had trouble hearing her. "I'm sorry," she croaked before she bolted for the stairs.

What is she apologizing for? She didn't do anything.

Noor watched Tya's retreating back for a moment before turning to Adam with a penetrating stare. "Is this true?

Adam nodded.

"And who told you to do this?" Noor addressed the question to Orri.

Orri lowered his eyes to the ground and answered, "No one."

Bending down Noor picked up the crystal dagger. His thumb traced the blade.

Adam could see the razor-sharp edge and his stomach clenched. How did I do that?

"Where did this come from?" Noor asked.

"I didn't mean to..." Adam glanced at Orri. The look on Orri's face stopped him from saying anything else.

Noor turned to Orri with eyebrows raised. "Do you have anything to add?"

Orri shrugged and looked at the horizon.

Adam shook his head and swallowed the lump in his throat, hoping Noor wouldn't question them further. What's happening to me? I could have hurt someone.

"I see." Noor's lips formed a grim line. "You were doing something you were not supposed to be doing, and it went wrong."

The sky went dark, plunging the rooftop patio into murky shadows. Adam stared into the inky black sky. There were no stars and no moon. The only light came from the glow of the crystal lamps on the street below.

"Sometimes the Time Crystal has an interesting sense of timing." Noor's voice almost sounded amused, but Adam couldn't be sure because the old man's face was in shadow.

"I think the council has underestimated all three of you." This time Noor's words were abrupt. Adam didn't need to see his face to know he was annoyed. "Try to stay out of trouble tonight. Get something to eat and then go to your room. We will deal with this tomorrow." Noor sighed audibly as he walked toward the stairs.

Adam ran his tongue over his dry lips. Noor's mad and Tya's upset. I'll never learn this stuff without their help. Maybe I can talk to Tya. His eyes flicked to Orri who stood with his arms crossed, staring at Noor's back. "We should find Tya. She's upset."

"She's a girl. They're always upset about something," said Orri. Adam could barely make out the rise of Orri's shoulders as he shrugged like he didn't care. Then he thought he saw Orri's hand reach up to his chest, where his skull pendant rested.

A moment later, Orri turned to Adam and casually draped an arm across his shoulders. His voice was warm and syrupy. "Look. You can make things easier for yourself if you stop trying to be better than me."

"Yeah, I can do that." Adam couldn't stop the words from coming out of his mouth. A cold shiver oozed down his spine, and he pulled out of Orri's reach.

Orri's confident voice continued. "I've been doing this a lot longer than you have and remember, I'm the hero Atlantis needs. Not you."

The hair on the back of Adam's neck stood up.

"Come on, we need to get to bed. Energy casting tires me out," said Orri.

He was beat too. As Adam followed Orri an uneasy feeling settled in his stomach. That was crazy, thought Adam. How did he make me agree with him?

He wanted to go home more than anything. To do that he had to save Atlantis. No way was he going to let Orri stop him.

Chapter Eleven

Noor descended the spiral staircase from the temple roof. Maybe Raine was right, and they should be worried. Orri was angry, and Adam was shifting forms with molecular transformation, an advanced skill he hadn't been taught. That kind of power comes with responsibility, and Noor knew Orri wouldn't have included that in the lesson.

His heart sat heavy in his chest as Noor made his way to the library. If the black cloud got much closer, his beautiful home would be destroyed. Noor worried about what he had done to contribute to the problem, and since Adam's arrival, his concern had only grown deeper.

Reaching the library, he walked between long rows of crystal skulls and stopped in front of a human-sized blue skull sitting on a stone stand. He laid his hand on top of the skull. The heavy wooden door behind the pedestal swung silently open.

Once inside, he closed the door and sat on one of the thirteen chairs around the circular table, an exact replica of the one in the council room. On this table sat nine crystal skulls as varied as the nine council members to whom they belonged. His skull, the thirteenth skull, was still safely hidden on Earth. The council had placed it there to prevent evil forces using it for their own purposes. Three more skulls would be added when the children finished their training.

Closing his eyes, he touched the thirteenth skull with his mind, reassuring himself his connection to it was still there. Unlike the other councillors, Noor was so old he relied on the link to his skull to stay alive.

Then his mind reached out to Raine and Alima. *Meet me in the safe room.* He sent the message as clearly as if he had spoken it out loud.

A few minutes later, Raine and Alima entered the chamber. Raine sat across from him. Alima passed by him and touched his shoulder before taking her place.

"I felt a rift in the energy field tonight," began Noor.

Alima frowned. "I felt nothing."

Raine leaned on the table. "Did you find out what caused it?"

"Orri, Tya and Adam were experimenting with shifting energy on the roof," Noor sighed. "Adam changed a crystal into a sharp knife, I believe by accident, and Orri almost hurt Adam with it."

"What?" Raine clenched his fist on the table. "I told you there would be trouble."

Noor rubbed his hand across his temple to ease the ache he felt there.

"Of course, he didn't mean to," Alima calmly stated. "The boy has only been here since yesterday. Perhaps we are expecting too much of him."

Noor stood up to pace the room. "Adam should not have the skill to change the form of an object yet, and Orri's anger at Adam being here could be a threat to the prophecy. It is not just the black cloud causing these problems, something evil has found a way into Atlantis." Had he done something evil? He shook his head to clear the thought and looked down at the other two. "It may have been a mistake to push their training to the next level. They are children. They are not mature enough to handle the responsibility of that level of magic."

"I understand your concerns." Alima nodded. "But Adam's powerful, youthful energy is what Atlantis needs. We must train him to control it." She stood up and squeezed Noor's hand. "It is possible we have missed something, but I want to believe that is not true. Orri will do what we need him to do." Her eyes crinkled at the sides. "Adam is our first priority. His energy is strong, but he must learn to control it. Then we can train him to use it."

The ache in Noor's chest eased a little as he gazed at her

confident face but fear still circled in his brain.

"Perhaps you can show him Atlantis through your eyes." The corner of Alima's mouth lifted. "And teach him how to do molecular transformation on himself, so he will understand it better. By doing that he will learn how to control what he senses."

"That is a good idea," agreed Noor. "I could show him our beautiful city. Will you bring Adam to my office tomorrow morning?"

"I am glad I could help. Adam will be there tomorrow." Alima grinned and waltzed out of the room.

"She thinks she is smarter than we are," said Raine.

"That is because sometimes she is." Noor felt a smile tug at his mouth.

When he was alone again, Noor collapsed onto a chair. The importance of what he had to do weighed heavy on his shoulders. He must train Adam in time to stop the black cloud and save Atlantis, but first he had to tell Adam who he really was.

He remembered his trip to Earth in the late 1970's of Earth's timeline. The council had sent him to hide the thirteenth skull and the crystal hand that Cavan had carved to join with the skull. Two separate locations for two artifacts to protect the powerful energy needed to move Atlantis. Somehow, he had to find a way to explain the results of that trip to Adam. Again, he reached out to the thirteenth skull for comfort and strength.

Chapter Twelve

The next morning, Alima showed Adam the way to Noor's office. He knocked on the door. Butterflies fluttered in his stomach. What was Noor going to say to him?

The door opened. "Come in," said Noor.

Crossing the threshold, Adam stared out a large window on the opposite wall. It flooded the small room with light, and had a stunning view of Atlantis. He could see the canal that circled the rise at the center of the city. Beyond that, another ring with buildings and green spaces. Then a canal and another circle of buildings. At the edge of the rings the deep blue ocean stretched to the horizon, where the black cloud loomed. It seemed bigger than it had looked yesterday.

Underneath the window sat a wooden table scattered with baseball sized skulls. Adam imagined sitting on the stool at the table and gazing out at Atlantis. That view would only continue to be there if he helped to save Atlantis. Adam looked away. He didn't want to picture what the scene would look like if he failed.

"Please sit down." Noor indicated two worn, overstuffed chairs facing each other.

Adam perched on the edge of the chair and rubbed his sweaty palms on his thighs.

Noor settled himself across from him. "I will talk to you, Tya and Orri about what happened on the roof later." Noor's eyes focused on Adam. "I have something else, something more important, I want to talk to you about now."

The butterflies in Adam's stomach twirled faster.

"Years ago, the council sent me to Earth to carry out a special mission. I have begun to think my time on Earth could be responsible for the black cloud reappearing." Noor's lips pinched together.

Adam didn't care about the cloud, he needed answers. "What did you do to cause that?"

"I lived on Earth for almost a year of your time. I made sure the council did not know exactly how long I was there, but someone from Atlantis cannot stay on Earth without causing problems with the timeline. At first, I did not see the changes because they were so small." Noor shook his head and gazed at Adam. "When I left Earth, I convinced myself I had caused no issues. It was during my time on Earth I met someone very special—your biological grandmother."

Noor's shoulders slumped. "Your mother had just been born, when I discovered I was in danger of causing permanent rips in the fabric of time."

"My mother? What are you saying?" Adam almost shouted.

Noor continued as if Adam had said nothing, "You came here wanting to return to your family. What you did not know, was that you have family here. It might be part of what brought you to Atlantis."

Noor gazed deeper into Adam's eyes. "I am your biological grandfather. Although it is true, I have no right to make the statement because I left Earth and abandoned the family I loved."

"No!" Adam jumped to his feet. "That can't be right."

"Please sit down." Noor placed a hand on his arm.

The last couple of days seemed to have had enough revelations to fill a year. This was too much to take in. Adam sank back onto the chair. "If you were my real grandfather you would have told me when I arrived," said Adam. "Or are you ashamed of me?"

"Oh, no!" Noor leaned toward him.

Adam sat back in his chair. He wanted no connection with the man in front of him. Something inside him snapped. "Yeah, when things got tough, you left." His mouth snapped shut, immediately regretting talking to Noor like that.

Part of Adam wanted to hear Noor's explanations, and part of him didn't want to hear anything the old man had to say. Curiosity won. "If you left when my birth mother was a baby— how do you know about me?"

"Because a foolish old man with regrets wanted to protect the child he loved." Noor's mouth formed a thin line. "I found out your mother and your father were looking for Atlantis. I was afraid the evil man who funded their expedition would hurt her. I went to Earth to warn her." Noor let out a long breath and continued. "Your mother was angry at me for leaving when she was a baby and would not listen to anything I said."

"Why are you telling me this now?" Adam's heart pounded so hard, it felt like it would jump out of his chest. His hands clenched the seat of the chair. "Do I really have to save Atlantis, or are you just getting me to fix your mistakes?" Adam spat the words out as if they caused a bad taste in his mouth.

"I did not bring you here..."

"She was right to be angry with you. You're a liar." Adam stood, unable to listen to any more. "I can't save Atlantis. I'm going home."

"If you go back to Earth now, Atlantis will be destroyed."

Adam stopped.

"The people who live here will die. Can you live with that?" Noor's eyes drilled into him.

He must still be lying. Adam stared at his feet to avoid Noor's penetrating gaze. But what if he wasn't?

As if the cloud was mocking him, the crystals on Noor's shelves rattled. Adam knew deep inside he couldn't have what he wanted. He couldn't change the past.

"I should have told you who I was sooner, but I cannot change the past," said Noor.

Adam looked up, surprised Noor's words echoed what he was thinking.

"I am so sorry," Noor said in a soft voice.

"Did I have a choice, in the beginning? Was I able to go home?"

"No. You came here because of the prophecy, and because of your real family connection to Atlantis." Noor sighed. "I could not bring myself to tell you when you were so upset and afraid, but I was wrong to ask you to choose without all the facts." The lines on his face were etched with sorrow. "I have to ask you to keep this between us for now. Alima, Raine and the rest of the council do not know what I have done."

"You want me to lie for you?" No, he wouldn't do it. It wasn't right.

Noor placed a hand on his arm. "There are members on the council who want to get rid of you. I am asking you to not say anything about this for your own protection."

It was true Orri and Cavan would love to see him gone, but Adam resented Noor saying he had to keep the secret for his own good. He pulled his arm away from Noor's grasp and his fingers curled into fists.

"I know what I did was wrong, but we have to wait for the right time to acknowledge what happened. It will be soon, I promise" said Noor.

Adam had kept his strange feelings hidden until now, so in a weird way he could understand what Noor was saying.

"Now, if you are ready, there is something I want to show you."

Chapter Thirteen

"I would like to take you on a trip." Noor's mouth tilted up.

"Where are we going?" Adam wasn't sure he wanted to go anywhere with Noor.

"Alima suggested I show you Atlantis. We are going to the outer ring of the city."

"I've already been there."

"True." Noor nodded. "But we will use energy to travel there."

"What if I do it wrong?" Adam sure didn't want a repeat of the roof incident.

"That is why we are going together, so I can teach you." Noor smiled a real smile. "I will be there to guide you. You remember the gate on the outer ring of the city where you entered Atlantis?"

"Sure...I guess." Adam gave half a shrug not feeling Noor's eagerness.

"Then let us begin." Noor stood up and held out his hand.

I'm too old for that. "Do I have to?"

"If I am connected with you, it is easier for me to guide you."

Adam reluctantly placed his hand in Noor's much larger one. The warm, rough palm comforted him. Maybe this wouldn't be so bad.

"Begin by tapping into your energy," Noor instructed. "Instead of projecting the energy out through your skull pendant, use the skull to magnify the energy within your body. When you are ready, visualize where you want to go and it will happen. I will be right by your side."

Adam felt a vibration from Noor's hand. It connected with the warmth in his belly. The feeling moved through him and swelled until it filled his entire being. His body shimmered and shifted. Something was happening. He closed his eyes and pictured the gate where he had first met Orri.

A panicked thought flashed in his mind. His dream. The tsunami.

A crack like thunder assaulted his ears and his eyes flew open. An acrid burning odor filled Adam's nose. Dust and smoke choked the air. The ground he stood on rolled under his feet.

Reaching out to clear the air in front of him he could barely see his hand. He coughed and sputtered, trying to breathe. Between gasps he stammered, "Where are we?"

"Hold on," Noor shouted over the omnipresent rumble that nearly drowned out all other noises.

Energy filled his body again. Adam wasn't sure what was shifting, him or the world around him. He gripped Noor's hand and closed his eyes, unable to think of anything.

Suddenly, the smell was gone. A floating sensation lifted his body. Afraid of what he might see this time, Adam squinted through half open eyes.

He was above a city, and looking down at rings of buildings separated by canals. Atlantis. They were...they were so high! Adam gasped and squeezed Noor's hand as hard as he could.

Forcing his gaze out to the horizon, he tried to swallow the huge lump of fear in his throat. A wall of thunderous black clouds loomed there. They cast a dark shadow on the ocean below. This viewpoint confirmed the cloud was much bigger than what he had seen yesterday. If there were any doubts with what Noor had said about the threat to Atlantis being real, they no longer existed.

The view before him flickered and disappeared.

His feet slammed into a solid surface. They were back in Noor's office. A fine grey dust covered the teacher, and he looked like a ghost. Looking down, Adam saw the same grey powder covered him too. "What...what happened?"

Noor staggered to the chair and sat down in a cloud of dust. After gasping for a few moments, he let out a small chuckle.

"What's so funny?" Adam's legs shook, and he wobbled over

to take a seat across from Noor.

"You are right. I should not laugh. But you must admit we look a little dishevelled."

"Where did we go?" Adam stammered. He didn't think the situation was funny at all.

Noor reached over and put a hand on top of Adam's. "Where do you think the outer ring of Atlantis is?"

He'd done it. It was his fault. "I knew where we were supposed to go. I pictured it. But just before we left, I saw my dream." Adam dropped his gaze to the floor.

"Your dream about the destruction of Atlantis," Noor asked in a soft voice.

Adam nodded. He glanced up expecting to see an angry Noor. Instead his grandfather's eyes were thoughtful and sad as they gazed at him.

"I should have warned you about the importance of focus. We landed in Atlantis just before the tsunami swept over it. Eleven thousand years ago."

"We went to the past?" Adam couldn't believe what he was hearing. "That's impossible! That's time travel!"

"It is possible to travel through time." Noor's voice was calm and steady. "Atlantis exists in the thirteenth dimension."

"Time travel? I did that?"

"Yes, you did." Noor nodded. "What you did was remarkable."

He did something remarkable. That was good, wasn't it? It sounded good, but Noor looked even more worried than he had before. "When we flew over Atlantis, did I do that too?"

"Hmm..." Noor's cheeks flushed. "Your time travel startled me. When we left ancient Atlantis, we landed above the present-day city instead of inside it. It is important to be focused and careful."

It was unsettling to think Noor could make so many mistakes, but not as scary as the growing mass of the black cloud. "Noor...why is the black cloud growing so fast?"

"Yes, it is growing but do not worry we still have time to save Atlantis." Noor gave Adam's hand a squeeze. "I am sorry I underestimated you, yet again. I promise you will learn how to use your energy properly and be able to help when the time comes." Noor straightened in his chair. "You should get cleaned up and have something to eat. Then you will need to rest to restore your energy."

"Okay," Adam agreed, but why was Noor not answering his question? What was he hiding from him now? Maybe if he asked in a different way. "Did the black cloud have anything to do with me time travelling?"

Noor frowned at him. "I do not think the black cloud made you do anything. The council will take care of protecting Atlantis, it is not your worry. I will teach you what you need to know. Now, can you find your room on your own?"

"Yeah, I think so," said Adam. Noor's answer didn't make him feel any better. Did that mean Noor was still lying, and the black cloud was about to destroy Atlantis because of him? Adam ground his teeth together to stop himself from saying anything else. If Noor wouldn't tell him the truth, then he had to figure it out on his own.

Chapter Fourteen

After Adam left, Noor shuffled along the hallway toward Alima's healing center, thankful that the boy had agreed to go to his room by himself. He was feeling every day of his eleven thousand-year-old age. There was a physical cost to energy work, especially when the time travel shouldn't have happened at all.

The council hadn't seen someone with Adam's talent for hundreds of years. He hoped the black cloud would hold back long enough for him to learn what he needed to.

"Do you think the boy was right about the negative energy of the cloud planting the memory of the dream?" Alima asked, after Noor told her what had transpired.

"No. No." Noor swiped at the dust on his face. "Most likely it was just his inexperience."

"We cannot rule out the fact that the cloud is growing." Alima's brow furrowed. "It is now visible on the horizon. People will get nervous. We need to act soon."

"Agreed." He nodded. "But we cannot have any more surprises. Especially when we try to move an entire city, inhabitants and all."

Alima led Noor to a chair and stood behind him, placing her hands on his shoulders.

Noor felt Alima's healing energy flow through his body like a gentle breeze. After all these years, it still amazed him how innate her restorative powers were.

"That should help." Alima gave his shoulders one last squeeze, and let go. "Get cleaned up, then Raine and I can help you come up with a plan."

Alima's confidence gave him hope. "That sounds good. Speaking of Raine, I should go apologize to him."

"Yes, you should." She gestured to his ash-covered robes. "Seeing you like this will give him an opportunity to gloat, and Raine likes to gloat."

✧✧✧

Noor opened the door to the lab and made his way through the crowded space to where his friend was working.

Raine looked up and raised his eyebrows. "Good trip?"

"Yes. We have just been eleven thousand years into the past." Noor sat on an empty lab stool beside Raine.

Raine pushed aside the skull he was studying. "Time travel. I did not think you were speeding up his lessons that fast."

"It was not the lesson I planned," Noor admitted.

"No?"

Noor ignored Raine's comment. "Adam initiated the time travel, but he is not the problem. It is us. We are the ones acting recklessly."

"As I told you."

Noor shrugged, conceding the point. "You were right. I came here to apologize for not listening."

Raine smiled. "Apology accepted."

"It has been a long time since I have seen the destruction of Atlantis, and it was a good reminder of what we are facing." Noor brushed the front of his tunic and dust wafted into the air. "Landing in the middle of a volcanic eruption certainly sparks the memory."

"You always had to learn things the hard way," said Raine.

"After I get cleaned up, we need to come up with a new plan. The black cloud is growing, and we have to teach all three children what they need to know before the city is lost."

"We will come up with a solution in time. We have to," Raine waved his hand at Noor. "Now get out of my lab before you get ash everywhere."

Chapter Fifteen

Adam headed for the room he shared with Orri. At least he hoped that was where he was going. Turning a corner, he saw Tya.

She rushed up, eyes wide. "What happened to you?"

"You're not mad at me?"

"It wasn't your fault." She twisted a strand of her long red hair around her finger. "I'm sorry, I shouldn't have let Orri talk us into doing that."

"Why are you sorry?"

"It's a long story. I don't want to talk about it. But it reminded me that energy..." Tya's voice waivered. She drew a deep breath before continuing. "That energy can be deadly and we must be very careful. What we did yesterday with Orri will never happen again. I won't let it." The corners of her lips moved up as if she wanted to smile but couldn't quite do it. "So, what happened to you?"

"I travelled with Noor. We went back eleven thousand years. I can time travel!" He stood a little taller.

"What are you covered in?"

"I'm not sure." He brushed a little of the fine powder from his shoulder. It felt soft, like baby powder. "There was dust everywhere. I couldn't see anything."

Tya touched Adam's sleeve and rubbed her fingers together. "It's not dust." Her eyes narrowed. "Where did you say Noor took you?"

"Noor didn't take us. I told you, it was me." Adam shrugged, trying to act like it was no big deal, even if Noor had told him he was remarkable. "We went back to when Atlantis was almost destroyed."

"To when the volcano erupted?" Tya touched his sleeve again. "You're covered in ash."

"It was an accident, but Noor didn't get upset."

"Noor hasn't taken *us* on a trip," Tya took a step back and frowned, her voice as harsh as Orri's.

"Hey, that's not fair!" How could she say that? Adam's jaw tightened. She was supposed to be his friend. "I don't want to be special, and you know it!"

Adam watched Tya's eyes widen. "Oh Adam, I do understand." She reached toward him but pulled away before she touched him. "It's just...time travel is really amazing. I've never done it, and I've never had a personal lesson with Noor."

Adam rubbed his palms down his thighs spreading ash everywhere. Tya was acting like, well, a girl. Adam shrugged. "Maybe I can teach you...I'm sure I know how to do it."

"Noor told us not to do transformations on our own." Tya's eyebrows lowered again.

"You're right." They were both quiet for a moment, lost in their own thoughts. Then something came to him, maybe Tya could help him find out if he caused the black cloud's growth. "I need to find out some information about the black cloud. Can you help me?"

She nodded. "Get changed and have a rest. Then I'll take you to my favorite place."

"Where's that?"

"You'll see." Tya walked away.

Some hallways were starting to look familiar to him, and Adam soon found his room. He got cleaned up and had some pancha. His bed called to him, as a wave of exhaustion pressed down on his body. He would lie down for a couple of minutes, and then go find Tya.

Chapter Sixteen

It was the middle of the night at the archeological site, but James couldn't sleep. Something kept telling him to go to the dig.

The weak shaft of light from the flashlight wobbled across the ground in front of him, making little impact on the darkness. The lack of illumination didn't slow him down, as he made his way across the site he knew so well. Reaching the current excavation, he climbed down the ladder into the pit. The pale beam revealed a grid of strings with several squares of dirt systematically dug out.

The thoughts were more insistent now, telling him where to dig, and to do it quickly. James grabbed a shovel and moved to an untouched area at the back of the grid.

He paused for a moment, terrified about destroying important evidence, but he couldn't resist the thoughts urging him on. Using the shovel, he attacked the ground, throwing chunks of soil over his shoulder with wild abandon.

He'd dug only a few inches, when he saw a glow emanating from the soil. Dropping the shovel, he dug frantically with his hands, unearthing the thing that had called him back to the site.

A crystal skull.

Later, James sat at his desk in the dull light of pre-dawn. In his dirty hands rested a beautiful, life-sized, clear crystal skull. The skull glowed, and rainbows danced across the ceiling, walls, and the stacks of papers on his disorganized desk.

How had Adrian Zador known the skull was hidden here? And how did he know James would find it? Even though Zador provided most of the funding for this dig, James knew the businessman couldn't be trusted with the skull. The fact Zador knew the skull existed, and had threatened James, meant this skull was very important to him.

"But why?" James muttered to himself. An artifact like this shouldn't be in such a primitive site. It must have been placed here by another, more advanced, civilization.

The skull warmed his palms. His fingers tingled, and the sensation flowed up his arms. It reminded him of holding his wife's hand.

His chest tightened. He still missed her so much. She had shared his passion for the fabled land of Atlantis. They had been looking for evidence of the lost empire while on vacation in the Caribbean, when she had died in a freak diving accident. That was twelve years ago. James hadn't had the heart to continue the work without her. He had stopped searching for the ancient empire and directed his efforts into other projects.

James took a deep breath, trying to ease the ache in his chest. He studied the skull. "You must have been here for a long time, but who concealed you is just as much a mystery as why you were buried here."

He was going crazy. Talking to himself. Or worse, talking to a skull. James shook his head. "All I know is, I need to protect you until I can figure out what you are and why I've found you."

He placed the skull on his desk. Nothing good could come of giving the artifact to Adrian Zador.

Grabbing his phone, he dialed his friend Matthew's number.

James frowned and stared at the phone in his hand. Why had he called Matthew? Matthew owned a store in Salem, Massachusetts. Then he remembered Matthew had studied crystal skulls for many years and was considered an expert in the field.

A rich male voice spoke. "Good afternoon, The Broom Closet," What was he going to tell him?

"Hello? Is anyone there?" asked the voice on the other end of the line.

"It's James." He paused, still not sure where to start. Taking a steadying breath, he tried again. "I'm not sure what made me call you. Strange things are happening here. I've found something." Watching the door to the office, James told him about the skull and how finding it made little sense.

"In my experience with skulls, you have to trust what you're feeling," Matthew said. "The skull is telling you to bring him to me for safekeeping."

"And I thought I was the crazy one." James laughed. "You can't expect me to believe this piece of crystal is telling me what to do?"

"One day, I'll teach you science doesn't explain everything. Bring the skull to me."

The door hadn't moved, and he could hear no sounds of anyone outside. Still...

"If Adrian Zador finds out what I've done, you might be in danger. I once saw him choke a man with one hand. The man almost lost consciousness, and Zador didn't care. He's dangerous."

"Bring the skull. I'll keep us all safe."

Hanging up the phone, James regarded the skull in front of him. "I hope you're happy. You're going to Salem."

A flash of golden light glowed deep inside the crystal skull.

Chapter Seventeen

Adam sat on the steps of the temple. His legs were drawn up to his chest and his chin was propped on his knees. He had slept longer than he meant to. It might be dark soon, but who knew when time was relative.

He was pondering where to look for Tya when someone tapped on his shoulder. Adam turned to see her looking down at him.

"You must be tired."

"A little. How do you know?"

"What happened with Noor wasn't simple energy casting. The more advanced the energy work, the bigger the physical drain on your body," Tya stated. "You can only do so much energy casting before you need to recharge. Don't worry, you'll learn to manage the side effects with more practice."

That explained why he felt so exhausted. Adam rubbed the toe of his sandal on the top step. "Am I ever going to learn this energy stuff, and be able to go home?"

"Listen." She touched his arm.

Adam felt the warmth of her hand through his sleeve. He liked the feeling.

"It must be really hard to learn what you're supposed to do in only a few days. We have prepared for this our whole lives."

Adam shrugged and continued to look at his feet. He didn't know how to respond to Tya's kind words.

"I can help you find out what you wanted to know," Tya gave his shoulder a little push. "Are you going to come with me or not?"

"I guess. So, where are we going?"

"The library."

And she's happy about this?

"What's fun about books?" Adam rolled his eyes. "I only read when I have to, for school."

Tya frowned at him. "What are books?"

"Books are in libraries back home. They tell you stuff." Adam stared back at her.

"Our knowledge is in crystal skulls." She laughed. "The skulls talk to you when you touch them."

"Like computers?"

Tya shook her head. "I don't know what you're talking about. Come on, I'll show you."

What did he have to lose? The crystal skulls sounded kinda interesting.

He fell into step beside Tya and glanced out of the corner of his eye at the drift of freckles across her cheeks. He'd never had a girl for a friend before.

Tya led Adam into the temple and down several long hallways. The grey stone floors and walls seemed to go on forever, twisting and turning in different directions. Some hallways were narrow. Some were wider with lots of doors and there were so many kinds of doors. Short, tall, fat, skinny, arched. Painted in a rainbow of colours, or shimmering with gold, copper or silver.

He was just figuring out how to find his way around the temple. What disturbed him was that the hallways were always empty. If he got lost, there didn't seem to be anyone around to ask for help. He had seen people on the streets. "How many people live in Atlantis?" he asked.

"Many years ago, there were over 50,000 people living in Atlantis. Now that Atlantis is in the thirteenth dimension there are only 1,853 including you," answered Tya.

Adam's brow wrinkled. "How do you know the exact number? And why would you include me?"

Tya smiled. "I like facts. Besides, I think you are part of Atlantis."

Adam shook his head. "Does everyone live in the temple?"

Tya chuckled. "Only a few of us live here. The council members and their families, the three of us, and the people needed to care for the building. Most people live in the city, including my parents." A sadness crept across her face. "I visit them as often as I can, but we are all busy doing what we're destined to do."

Adam's chest ached. He missed his parents but he couldn't imagine not being able to live with them. "Why do you stay here?"

"Because I'm training, so that one day I will be a part of the council. Everyone has a job, and each person has a level of energy casting allowing them to do their jobs." Tya sounded like a teacher reciting information she considered important. "Some provide food and pancha, like my parents, some convert energy to light the city, some purify water for us to drink, some fix the buildings and the roads. And some, like us, make sure Atlantis is safe."

"You mean not everyone can do what we do?" Adam asked.

Tya shook her head "Of course not. We have a special talent."

Adam swallowed hard. He wasn't sure he liked being special, it was no different from being weird.

They stopped in front of a door guarded by a very large man. His dark blue tunic stretched across his chest. The sheer size of him would have been frightening, except for the huge grin splitting his wide face.

"Back again so soon?" he asked.

"I need more information and I missed your cookies." Tya smiled. "Adam, this is Horatio. He protects the library."

"Nice to meet you, Son of Earth. It's your first time here, isn't it?"

Adam nodded.

"You're in for quite a treat. Come in." He leaned down and opened the door, handing Adam a cookie as he passed. Horatio beamed and gave a cookie to Tya. "I always have cookies for you."

Tya grinned at him and took a bite of her cookie.

Adam and Tya passed through the door into another hallway.

They moved down the long corridor. Wooden doors flanked both sides of the passage. Shiny gold double doors stood at the end, glowing in the soft light overhead.

"Why is the library guarded?" Adam asked.

"The library holds all our knowledge. It is guarded in many ways, because the council worries about dark energy causing something bad to happen to it."

"Bad things happen on Earth, too. Wars and terrorist attacks are scary."

"Your world sounds so strange..."

A tall girl, maybe a little older, stepped out of a door, interrupting Tya.

"Hi, Caileen," Tya said with a big grin.

The girl had a long face with a strong chin and a wide, smiling mouth. "I'm glad you're here. I want to talk to you about..." Her words slipped into silence when she noticed Adam.

"Adam, this is Caileen. You've met her father, Cavan. He's the librarian," said Tya.

A smile lit up Caileen's face. "Hi, Adam. It's nice to meet you. I'm glad you're here to help Atlantis." She gestured toward the door at the end of the hall. "Our library is amazing. I can give you a tour if you like."

Adam shrugged. "Sure." Another girl who thinks the library is amazing. *Really?*

Adam heard the entrance door to the library open again. He turned to see Orri walking toward them. What was he doing here?

"We were just about to show Adam the library," said Caileen as if seeing Orri in the library was normal. "Do you want to come with us?"

"Sure." Orri didn't look like he wanted to be there, until he stood beside Caileen and smiled down at her.

So, there is someone that Orri likes.

Caileen and Orri lead the way to the double doors, with Adam and Tya trailing behind.

The sounds of a large crowd escaped from the other side of the doors. As he got closer to the end of the hall, the voices got louder and louder. Then the doors opened. There were no people, but the noise thundered in his head.

The cookie fell from his hand as Adam clamped his palms over his ears but the cacophony still didn't let up.

"Make it stop!" Tya, Orri and Caileen's lips were moving but he couldn't hear what they were saying. Unbearable pain assaulted his ears. He squeezed his eyes shut and tightened his whole body.

The clamour ceased suddenly, as if someone had shoved two pillows over his ears. Adam opened his eyes one at a time. He stood beside Horatio at the entrance to the library.

"Hey, young Adam. Leaving so soon?"

"I don't...I don't know." Adam took a deep breath to steady himself. "I tried to stop the noise, and now I'm here. I don't know what happened."

"You look a little shaky. Just sit down and take 'er easy," said Horatio.

Adam slid onto the bench beside the door and took another deep breath, trying to stop his hands from trembling. The pain had stopped, but how had he ended up here?

Horatio stood next to Adam and clasped his hands in front of his chest.

Tya burst through the door with Orri and Caileen right behind her. "There you are! Are you okay?"

Before Adam could say anything, Noor also stood in front of him. Adam wondered how the old man had arrived at the library just then.

"Tell me what happened," Noor said in a strong but gentle voice.

Adam tried to piece together the sequence of events. "I heard a loud noise in the hallway. I didn't know what it was. When we got closer to the doors, it got louder."

A puzzled look crossed Tya's face. "What noise?"

Orri scowled at him.

Adam shrugged. "Like...I don't know. It sounded like a bunch of voices, all yelling at once. The doors opened and my ears felt like they were going to explode."

"But, no one's in the library," Caileen said.

A look of relief replaced the worry in Noor's eyes.

"I closed my eyes, and when I opened them I was here. Please, believe me," pleaded Adam.

"I understand. Nothing is wrong," said Noor.

It felt serious. Adam stared into the old man's eyes, searching for any hint he wasn't telling the truth.

Noor smiled and extended his hand toward Adam. "Take my hand and we will open the door together."

I hope this goes better than the last time I held his hand, thought Adam. He hesitated for a moment and then placed his hand in Noor's much larger one. The warmth from Noor's hand flowed up Adam's arm and into his brain, calming his agitated thoughts. They walked down the hallway, followed by the others.

Adam heard the noise again, this time a low buzzing instead of a loud rumble. Noor's grip tightened and another soothing wave entered his body, muting the buzzing noise. As they continued walking, the noise only got a little louder. He could hear the sound, but it wasn't deafening or painful.

They paused in front of the doors. Noor nodded, and they opened. Before them was a great hall filled with shelves of crystal skulls in different colours and sizes. No one was there, but the skulls were talking. All of them, at once.

Adam focused on a large green skull.

Long ago when Atlantis existed in South America, Machu Picchu was the city's hidden location...

His eyes darted to the small pink skull next to the green one.

"The Thirteenth Dimension is the state of being..."

Further down, a large clear skull caught his gaze. In a rough voice it ground out the words one at a time. *"Of the pieces, there are three. The hand, the skull and..."* Adam couldn't be sure if the skull's words or its grating voice caused him to shudder.

"It's the skulls. They talk." Adam's bright voice didn't quite cover up his discomfort. "And they all say something different."

"That is what I suspected." Noor tilted his head. "This ability of yours can be annoying. In Atlantis, crystal skulls hold our knowledge. Each skull contains a separate part of our wisdom. As you can see there are thousands of skulls."

Adam nodded. He gazed at the rows and rows of shelves reaching up high above his head and stretching away from him as far as he could see.

"The sound of that many skulls speaking at once can be deafening. Most people need to touch a skull to hear what it has to say. You and I hear the skulls without touching them." Noor smiled. "It is a skill only a few of us have. Now, to manage the voices, you need to send the energy flow to your ears. By turning the energy up or down you can choose how much you want to hear."

Focusing his energy, Adam could make the noise get louder and quieter. "I get it. It's like the volume control on the TV."

"I have not thought about television in years, but if it helps you understand what to do, that is good."

He could do something Noor could do. A warmth spread through his chest as Noor's words sunk in. "But how did I end up back at the entrance?" He looked up at Noor. "Did the skulls do that?"

"No, they did not. You did."

"How?"

"You did molecular transformation on yourself." Noor's eyes narrowed and his lips flattened as he turned toward the others. "As you are all here, there is something I would like to address."

Chapter Eighteen

Noor stared at Adam. "Based on our travels this morning, I know it was molecular transformation you three were experimenting with on the roof."

A lump formed in Adam's throat. Avoiding Noor's eyes, he nodded.

"I am disappointed in all three of you," Noor scowled at Tya and Orri. "You both know how dangerous it can be. One of you could have been injured or killed." His eyes flicked to Adam then turned back to the other two. "You are not to do molecular transformations again without supervision. Am I clear?"

"Yes." Tya's voice quaked. "We've learned our lesson." She turned and eyed the two boys.

Adam nodded, too. Clenching his jaw, he watched Orri. He wouldn't have been involved if it wasn't for the older boy's persuasion.

Orri nodded in agreement, but his face showed no emotion.

"Good." Clearing his throat, Noor continued in a gentler voice. "Adam, take this opportunity to learn a little about the library from Caileen, Orri and Tya. I will talk to you later."

Adam bobbed his head again, relieved that Noor didn't seem angry anymore.

After Noor left, Tya said, "I hate it when Noor is mad at us." She glared at Orri. "I won't let you talk me into breaking the rules again."

"You stayed," said Orri. "You could've left."

"I won't do that again either," said Adam, hoping Orri wouldn't be able to persuade him differently.

Orri's hand reached up to rub his skull pendant, his eyes darkened and in a soft voice he asked, "Are you blaming me too?"

A chill skittered down Adam's spine. "No, I'm not."

"That's not what it looks like, Earth boy."

"We all know better now," said Tya.

Orri shrugged. "If I have to break the rules to save Atlantis, I'll do it." A smile flitted across his face when he gazed at Caileen. "You don't need me for the tour. I'll talk to you later."

Adam watched Orri leave. The only reason the older boy had come to the library was to see Caileen. He wondered if they were more than just friends.

Caileen gestured to a rack of skulls just inside the library doors. "Would you like me to explain the index system we use?"

Even though Adam didn't think he would ever need it, he nodded anyway. He noticed the skulls on the rack were all the same, white quartz and small enough to fit in the palm of his hand.

"These skulls are linked to all the other skulls in our library. They will point you to the right section when you ask them a question." Caileen rubbed her chin for a moment. "What is popollama?" she asked, and smiled at Adam.

A skull on the bottom shelf glowed and lines in the stone floor lit up showing the way.

Caileen followed the lines. After going down a couple of aisles and turning two or three corners, they stood in front of a glowing dark green skull.

"Popollama is a ball game." Adam heard the skull say. *"The ball is never allowed to touch the ground. Players can't hold or even touch the ball with their hands - only the head, elbows, knees, hips, and shoulders are used to move the ball down the field. The object is to get the ball through the stone hoop. This is extremely difficult, so when it happens the game is over."*

"Sounds like soccer and basketball combined. It would be fun to try it," said Adam.

"Orri is obsessed with it. Anytime you can't find him he's on the popollama field," commented Caileen.

"Do you know why Orri hates me?" Adam asked.

Caileen pressed her lips together. "It's not you he's mad at."

Adam snorted. "You could have fooled me."

"Orri's mother disappeared when he was twelve. No one knows what happened to her. It changed him." Caileen sighed. "He believes that if he does everything right, she'll come back. And that's the reason he thinks he should be the one to save Atlantis."

Adam nodded. Orri was still a jerk, but now he knew why.

"Let's continue with the tour," said Tya, a little too enthusiastically. "Once you learn where the different sections are, you'll be able to ask questions without going back to the index skulls."

Tya's obsession is the library, thought Adam.

Caileen and Tya led him between the rows of skulls, both telling him what they liked about the library. Tya had forgotten about researching the black cloud.

Adam didn't listen to the girls. He was too busy experimenting with his energy volume control.

"Dark energy grows every day." said a large purple and black skull.

Adam stopped. What does that mean? If dark energy is always growing, even if I save Atlantis, it won't stay safe for long.

"Hurry up," Tya said, from further down the aisle.

"Come here." Adam beckoned her.

She and Caileen returned. "What's up?"

"Listen to that skull." Adam pointed. "What does it mean – dark energy is growing every day?"

Both Tya and Caileen placed their hands on the skull to hear what it had to say.

Caileen pulled her hand away. "The skull explains that dark energy is always growing, because the universe is always expanding. Light energy grows too, and balances the dark energy." Her brow puckered. "In the thirteenth dimension, when someone uses energy for corrupt purposes, the prophecy says the dark energy will grow faster than the light energy, and there will no longer be a balance between them."

"Using energy for corrupt purposes," Tya murmured. "I

thought so."

"But who is doing it? And how?" Adam prayed he wasn't responsible.

"I don't know," replied Caileen.

"The black cloud you saw on the horizon is the physical form of dark energy imbalance," Tya commented.

"Okay, dark energy and the cloud are connected, and the cloud is getting bigger," said Adam. He didn't trust Caileen enough to admit how much the cloud had grown. Instead he asked, "How much time do we have?"

"The fact the cloud is visible means we don't have a lot of time," Caileen said in an urgent voice.

"What will happen when it's too late?" Adam held his breath.

"When the cloud is above us it creates chaos with the natural forces. The earthquakes and tremors are just the beginning. Tsunamis will form in the ocean, and volcanic eruptions from deep within the earth will rise to the surface." Caileen shook her head. "Atlantis must move before the cloud is completely over the city, or we'll be destroyed."

The cloud would be here soon. A sickening feeling settled in Adam's stomach. What if he had caused this?

A wave of exhaustion slammed into him. He reached out to steady himself, and his hand landed on Tya's shoulder.

"Adam, what's wrong?" Her arm wrapped around his back, and stopped him from crumbling to the floor.

Caileen placed a hand on his forehead. "His energy levels seem low."

"How do you know that?" Adam croaked.

"My mother was a healer, and I inherited some of her skills." Caileen moved to prop him up on the other side. "You're not used to all this energy casting. We'll help you to your room. A full night's sleep should get you back to normal."

By the time the girls got him to his bed, Adam could barely place one foot in front of the other.

Chapter Nineteen

Adam hardly remembered getting to his room the night before. But when he got out of bed this morning, none of the fatigue from the day before remained. Caileen had been right.

Somehow, with all that had happened yesterday, Adam still hadn't found out if the black cloud was growing because of him. Maybe today, with Tya's help, he could answer the question. He put on clean clothes, grabbed some pancha, and headed for the library.

Adam was confident he knew where he was going. Despite that, several hallways later he stood at the entrance to the council room, nowhere near the library. How did I get here?

Noor sat alone in the room with his back to the open door. Adam didn't want to bother him, and was about to turn around, when he noticed Noor's hand. Blue and white flames leaped from his mentor's palm. The flames flickered and danced. Before Adam could run to help him, the fire twisted and rolled into a ball of blue light. The ball floated, darkened to a deep blue and then changed into a shiny black feather.

Adam held his breath as he watched the spectacle.

The black feather morphed into a beautiful purple crystal, then a glistening white conch shell. A dozen white feathers flew out of the conch shell, and it disappeared. The feathers rose, fluttering then separating as they turned in the air. Noor swept his arm in a wide arc and the feathers circled the room, coming back to stand in a stack above his hand. Then they dropped one by one into his palm. Closing his fingers, he lowered his hand.

Noor's forehead furrowed as he stared across the table. Not

wanting to look like he was spying, Adam ducked out of sight and tiptoed back the way he had come before Noor could see him. What was Noor doing? It looked so cool.

Eventually Adam found the door to the library. "Is she in there?" he asked knowing Horatio knew who he meant.

The guard chuckled. "Of course." He opened the door and handed Adam a cookie.

Adam munched on the cookie as he walked down the aisles between the tall stacks of skulls. The library smelled fresh and clean, like the air outside after a rain shower, not like the musty, booky smell of a library on Earth. He felt more comfortable in this library. It was crazy. He must've been hanging around with Tya too much.

In the middle of the library he found her sitting at a table with half a dozen skulls on it. She looked up and smiled. "Hi."

"Hi," Adam replied as he slipped into the chair across the table from her. "On the way here, I saw something." He told her what he witnessed in the council chamber.

Tya smiled. "Noor was just playing with energy. My Nan used to say it was a relaxing thing to do." Tya took a deep breath and a glimmer of a smile moved across her mouth. "When Atlantis is safe, it might be fun to try."

"That would be cool." Adam leaned forward. "I need to talk to you about something that happened when Noor and I travelled to the outer edge of the city. When we came back, we ended up way above Atlantis. The black cloud has grown. It's a monster storm cloud now."

"I noticed it was bigger when I was coming here."

"It's huge." Adam spread his arms wide trying to show what he saw.

Tya pulled at her lip. "Did Noor see it?"

Adam nodded. "He said not to worry about it, but...I'm pretty sure it bothered him." Adam clasped his hands together on the table and leaned in. "I think it's growing because of me."

"Why would you think that?" Tya shot him a quizzical look.

"As soon as I arrived, the cloud appeared on the horizon. Now look at it."

"I don't think you are the problem, but we need more information about dark energy before we can figure it out."

"How do we do that?"

Tya gestured to the skulls around them. "We're in the best place to find the answer. Give me a couple of minutes." She rushed off.

Adam gazed at the stacks of shelves encircling the small open area. Each shelf held dozens of crystal skulls in many sizes and colours. The voices of the skulls were now just a low hum in Adam's head.

It was fun looking at an individual skull and turning up the volume to hear what information the skull held. He played with several skulls, and then he focused on a small green skull. It said, *the Great Crystal has been lost for thousands of years.*

"We have a problem." Tya plopped down in the chair next to him. "Most of the information I think we need is in the vaults. We aren't allowed down there."

"Then how do we find out what's happening with the cloud, and what we're supposed to do about it?"

Tya drew her eyebrows together. "Maybe Caileen can help. She's a library assistant and has more access to the library than I have."

"But Cavan's her father," argued Adam. "We don't want him to know about this, either. He's just creepy, and he doesn't like me."

"Caileen's my friend. She'll help us and keep our secret."

"Hi." Caileen appeared from behind a row of skull-laden shelves.

Had she been spying on them? Adam hoped she hadn't heard what he had said about her father.

"We were just talking about you," Tya smiled at Caileen. Her voice dropped to a whisper. "We need to find out if the cloud is growing because of Adam. But we don't want to tell anyone on the council until we can figure it out. Can you help us?"

"Why would you think the black cloud and Adam are connected?" asked Caileen.

"Because the black cloud has grown in the last couple of days since Adam arrived," said Tya. "He says it's grown a lot."

"I know we can see it on the horizon now. And you believe your arrival has something to do with it?" Caileen voice got quieter and her gaze narrowed in on Adam. "Are you sure?"

"Like you didn't hear us talking about it already." Adam leaned back and crossed his arms.

"Stop it, Adam." Tya scowled at him. "We can trust her."

"You and Orri are so much alike," Caileen said with a knowing smile.

Adam clenched his jaw.

"It's a compliment." Caileen joined them at the table. "But I suppose you wouldn't see it that way. You both are so focused on your own goals, that you question everyone else's motives." She leaned on her elbows. "I heard you talking because I was nearby in the library. That is why I came over here, but I didn't hear what you were saying."

She seemed sincere, but Adam still wasn't sure he could trust her, because Cavan had made it very clear how much he wanted to get rid of him.

"Look," she said. "I'm happy you came to Atlantis because I didn't want to be trained as a part of the Three. I was willing to do it," Caileen shrugged, "but it never felt right. I have mixed energy. I'm from the People of the Sky on my mother's side, and from the People of the Earth on my father's side. It's harder for me to use energy, as my talent isn't grounded in one element. Your lineage is pure and that's why it's your destiny to help save Atlantis, not mine. There are other ways I can help Atlantis."

"What does 'my lineage is pure' mean?"

"You are a Son of Earth, and your whole family is from the People of the Earth," answered Tya. "Someone in your family passed the ability to work with energy to you."

He knew that someone was Noor, but he'd promised not to say anything. "I was adopted when I was three months old," he told her tersely.

"Someone in your birth family must have been able to work with energy," said Caileen. "That is where you got your abilities from."

"My Nan passed her skills to me." A sad look passed across

Tya's face. "She was a council member."

Caileen touched Tya's hand and Tya blinked hard.

Adam looked from one girl to the other. Something had just happened between them, he didn't know what it was, but thankfully it had turned their attention away from his family ties.

"The black cloud is growing," he said hoping to bring the conversation back to the original problem, "but Noor said we still have time."

"If the cloud is that close, we have more to worry about than what caused the dark energy to grow," said Caileen. "We must bring the thirteenth skull home."

"The thirteenth skull? What's that?" asked Adam

"It's Noor's energy-focusing skull. It was secretly hidden on Earth decades ago, to protect its energy from being used for evil purposes," Caileen answered. "Each of the councillors, including Noor, has a skull, and Noor's skull unites all the skulls so they can move Atlantis away from danger. Someone needs to get the thirteenth skull from Earth."

"But we can't go to Earth." Adam narrowed his eyes at her.

"Well, that's not true..." Caileen tilted her head to one side.

"What? Are you kidding me?" Adam threw his hands up. "We can go there?"

"Be quiet. Someone might hear you." Tya looked over her shoulder.

Adam could see the skull lined aisle was empty.

"It's not that easy," she said. "We can't do it without permission from the council."

"Why?"

"Travelling outside Atlantis is restricted," Caileen said, her long blond hair falling forward as she leaned toward him. "And it has to be approved by the council because of the damage it can cause."

Adam frowned. "What damage?"

"You need to understand how time works," Caileen explained. "Time on Earth only moves in one direction, but our time is more fluid than Earth's. That is why the time you spend here is not noticed on Earth."

"I still don't understand." Adam spat the words through gritted teeth. He could have gone home any time? All other thoughts were blocked out. Noor had lied to him again. They had all lied to him!

Chapter Twenty

"I forget how little you know of our world. It's like..." Caileen pressed her lips together for a moment, and then continued. "Every time we travel from Atlantis to Earth, we cause a snag in the fabric of time. If there are too many holes, we alter the timeline on Earth. Atlantis can be affected too, but we can repair the problems in Atlantis. We are unable to fix Earth's time stream."

"What does that mean?" Adam's voice rose again. Why couldn't someone just tell him the truth?

"Shhh! It means we could change the future on Earth, maybe even change your future."

Adam didn't raise his voice this time. Instead, he said the words very slowly. "Can I travel to Earth or not?"

"You can't do it without a council member's help. And even with their help, it's a bad idea." Caileen's lips formed a thin line. "Even if you went you couldn't stay there, because with each person who sees you, the chances of causing a snag in time grows enormously."

"So, I'm never going home." Adam rose and leaned on the table.

"Caileen didn't say that," Tya corrected him in a stern voice. "Noor said once the prophecy is fulfilled, there would be a way. I believe him. You can't go now." Her eyes drilled into him.

Adam wished she wouldn't look at him like that. He exhaled noisily. "Someone has to go to Earth to get this skull, don't they?" He looked from Caileen to Tya. "Why couldn't it be us?"

"No," said Tya. "We don't know where the skull is and how much time we have before the cloud is over us. Let me and

Caileen check into it and then we can go to the council."

"You don't understand." The muscles in his jaw tightened.

"I do." She laid her hand on his arm.

Adam pulled away.

"Don't be like that," Tya pleaded. "You will get home. Noor promised."

Adam looked at both. They didn't get it. They had never been yanked away from their homes. Told they couldn't get back. And then found out they could get home after all. Who cared about the fabric of time? "Yeah, whatever."

He turned away, but before he could take a step, Tya spoke in a quiet voice.

"Adam?"

He glanced over his shoulder.

"You won't do anything crazy, will you?"

Adam snorted. "Me. No way."

Tya followed him down the aisle. "Please don't try anything by yourself. We'll figure this out."

Tya's calm sensible voice echoed his mother's advice of 'Don't go into the water by yourself". He'd ignored his mom, and look at the trouble he'd gotten into.

I can go home. The thought filled his mind, and his toes curled in anticipation of stepping into the warm sand of a Caribbean beach. It would feel so good to step onto the beach for a couple of minutes.

Why can't I have a choice? Atlantis had blocked him from going home at every turn. Now the pull to go home wasn't going away. He didn't care if he was to blame for the black cloud threatening Atlantis. He didn't care that he needed to be trained to save Atlantis. He would not be stopped this time.

But I don't know how to get there. He couldn't mess up again. Maybe he wasn't sure how to travel to Earth, but he'd bet Tya knew what to do. He *had* to convince her to show him how. It wasn't like he wouldn't come back. He'd promised to help Atlantis. His dad taught him to always keep his promises. The thoughts of his dad made homesickness wash over him again. I've got to go home.

Adam turned around. "Now that I know I can go home, it is all that I can think about, I must go there."

"You can't! You have to help Atlantis," Tya hissed. "We need you here."

"I know I can't stay there." Adam's fingers curled into fists. "I need to know I can do this." His eyes drilled into Tya's. "Please show me how." He rushed on. "There's a small, out-of-the-way beach I can go to. No one will see us."

"No! We got into trouble before for using magic without supervision." Tya paced back and forth.

"We need to practice, don't we? Noor said that was important, too." She had to agree, she just had to.

"You don't understand." Tya stuffed her hands into her pockets. "Like Noor said, if something goes wrong, we could get hurt or worse..." She pulled a stone out of her pocket. The purple rock was the same size and shape as a large coin. Tya rubbed her thumb back and forth across it.

"That won't happen. I told you we won't see anyone!" Adam clasped his hands in front of his chest. "Atlantis and Earth are connected, haven't you ever wanted to see Earth?"

"I wanted to see the pyramids in Mexico." Her eyes pooled with tears. "But not anymore."

What did I say? "Tya don't cry." Adam reached toward her but she took a step back before he could touch her.

"I'm not." She swiped at her face and returned her gaze to the stone in her palm. "We were studying the Mayans. Something went wrong." Her voice dropped to a whisper. "And my Nan died." Tya shook her head. "I think I might have done something to cause it. I can't let anything like that happen again." She rubbed the purple stone harder.

"What is that?" Adam pointed at the stone in her hand.

"It's called a worry stone. My Nan gave it to me." Tya sniffed and closed her eyes. "It's the only thing I have to remember her by."

"I'm sorry." Adam swallowed hard. He couldn't imagine what his life would be like without his grandmother. He knew now he had no hope of changing her mind. He'd have to get to Earth on his own.

Tya let out a shaky breath. "Caileen and I will check into the dark cloud. It won't take us long to find enough information to convince the council they need to act now."

Adam nodded knowing she was deliberately changing the subject.

Tya gave him a crooked half smile. "I learned so much from my Nan about our ancient history. Atlantis has survived many challenges. I'm sure we'll make it this time."

"That's great." Adam smiled too. The brittleness of the fake expression pulled at his cheeks. "I'm going back to my room. Come get me when you're ready." He turned away.

"Adam?"

Adam stopped with his back to Tya. He didn't think he could pull off another smile.

"You will get home. You know that, don't you?"

"Sure. See you later." He strode away from her before she could say anything else. Turning down another aisle Adam stopped and leaned against the shelves.

Dimensions 10, 11 and 12 are the consciousness of the creators and the 13th dimension, where Atlantis exists, is beyond that.

Adam had no idea what the skull was talking about. He straightened and studied the sky-blue crystal skull on the shelf by his ear. He'd spent enough time in the library that he automatically muted the chatter from the skulls. He hadn't considered the knowledge they held. *Stupid.* He was standing in the one place in Atlantis where he could find out how to travel to Earth. And the idea hadn't crossed his mind. "How do I travel to Earth," he asked.

Lines in the floor lit up. He followed them until he stood in front of a life-sized pink crystal skull.

Travelling to Earth from an energy casting point of view is very similar to any other form of travelling. But crossing inter-dimensional lines can have serious consequences.

Adam concentrated on the skull. He skipped over the consequences to get to the travelling directions.

To begin travelling, feel your energy. Magnify it in your body.

The familiar vibrations swirled in his body. He closed his eyes, and lost himself in the warmth radiating throughout his being.

Concentrate, the skull said sounding exactly like Noor. *Imagine where you want to go. It is most important to see every detail clearly in your mind.*

He conjured up an image of the beach. He saw the teal blue ocean, heard the sound of the waves washing up on the white sand, and smelled the salty water. Exactly as it had been the last time he was there. Something brushed his hand. The world around him flickered and disappeared into total darkness and empty silence.

A rustling sound, like leaves in the wind, trickled into the stillness. A cool draft of air lifted him off the ground and pushed him forward. Far ahead, a pinpoint of light disrupted the darkness. The wind became warmer and stronger, moving him faster and faster. The sound grew into a raging storm and the light grew. The wind bucked and twisted, tossing him about.

Adam slammed into something solid. Breath whooshed out of his body.

Gasping, he tried to suck air into his heaving chest. The movements sent pain flooding through him.

I need air, his body screamed. He attempted a small shallow breath. There was less pain. Good. He drew another small breath and another, and eventually oxygen moved into his body again.

Dimness. Was it night? He'd imagined the beach in daylight. His eyes adjusted to the gloom. A pool of dark water was surrounded by rough stone walls reaching overhead to form a roof. A shaft of light streamed down into the water through a small crack above.

This wasn't the beach. A knot formed in Adam's belly.

Chapter Twenty-One

How did he end up in a cave?

At least he wasn't under water. The only sound was the occasional drip of water from the roof.

"Help!" His voice echoed again and again in the chamber, the noise pounding on his ears. The last echo of sound died, and the stillness returned.

He was alone. The reality of his situation crushed down on him. Sweat seeped down his spine. There was no one to help him.

A ripple formed at the far edge of the pool and moved toward him. He raised one hand to shield his eyes and look past the ray of light. Squinting, he saw something thin shoot out of the water. It thrashed silently back and forth. A tentacle from some water monster? No, it was an arm. A waving human arm.

He wasn't alone. Tension slid out of his body for a moment before it slammed back into him. Who was it? How did they get into the cave? Why were they there?

The figure shook the water from its long red hair. The movement played out in a strange silence. Adam peered at the face. Tya? Tya!

He stepped toward her, but the left half of his body refused to move. Looking back over his shoulder for the first time he saw his arm, part of his chest and one leg were trapped within the rock. He could feel them, painless and still attached to his body, but they were inside the wall of the cave.

Pushing hard into the ground with his free foot, he yanked his chest forward, grunting with the effort. Pain shot through him, but the rocks held fast. He yelled to Tya, "Help! I'm trapped."

Again, the sound of his own voice came back and assaulted him. Tya waved again, still treading water, her mouth opened as if she was calling, but she made no sound.

Why couldn't he hear her? Pain shot through his chest that had nothing to do with the rocks that trapped him. He needed help.

Then a thought, not his, popped into his head. *Can you hear me?*

Who's there?

Adam, it's me, Tya.

Tya? In my head? How?

I can hear your thoughts, and you can hear mine. I've learned about this, but I've never done it before.

I listen to skulls this way, but I didn't know people could do it. He smiled, despite his situation. *I'm so glad you're here. But...how did you get here?*

I thought you might try to travel on your own, so I followed you. I touched your hand to get your attention...but it was too late. You travelled and brought me with you.

Oh Tya, I'm sorry. Adam wanted to go to her. *It'll be okay.*

What have we done?

Her thoughts sounded scared. Adam knew she was thinking about her Nan. *I didn't mean to drag you with me. We'll find a way out of this.* He hoped his words were true.

I hope so, she replied.

I need your help, said Adam.

I'll be right there. Tya swam to shore and pulled herself up. Her body stopped short and flopped backward into the water. Rising carefully this time, and rubbing a spot on her head, she extended her hand. Her palm flattened like a mime pushing against a pretend wall.

I found what's blocking our voices. Her eyes focused on him. *Adam! What happened?*

I don't know. Tya, I'm scared.

Hold still. Let me try to move this invisible wall. She strained against it with both hands. *I can't budge it. I'm going to try shifting it with energy.* A small frown formed on her face as she concentrated. This time she was lifted off her feet and thrown much further into the water. Climbing out again, she stood and pushed her sopping hair off her face. *Well, that didn't work. Do you have any ideas?*

Adam shook his head, and swallowed hard against the lump forming in his throat.

She squinted at him. *Can you use energy to move your body?*

I can't...I can't think.

Sometimes your strength is not something big, it's just a tiny whisper that says, "You got this!" I know you can do it.

Tya's confident thoughts were hard to resist. *Okay, okay, I'll try.* Adam reached deep inside himself to find the energy. The vibrations began, but only the half of his body outside the wall sensed what was taking place. He focused on moving out of the wall but his body remained where it was. He shook his head. *I can't do it. I'm stuck.*

Try doing molecular transformation, thought Tya.

Actually dissolving my body, not just moving it. Are you crazy?

You've done it before.

That didn't work out so well. What if I change myself into something else like I did with the crystal? This was his body Tya was talking about changing.

You've learned what to do since then. If you can stay calm you'll be fine, she insisted.

Easy for you to say. You're not the one trapped in a wall. I'm not calm.

There's no other way. Just breathe. You've got this, Tya coached.

I can't do that. His body shook. The quivering moved from his free limbs to those trapped inside the wall.

A memory of Raine's voice flowed into his mind. You are Son of Earth. Draw energy from your element.

That was it. Rock was an Earth element. Energy surged into him from the wall.

He disintegrated. He tried to move his body but there was nothing to move. The physical Adam did not exist. He was free flowing molecules with no form. He could see, hear, feel...nothing.

Knowing he needed to shift, body or no body, all his thoughts yelled. *Move.*

Something was happening. A trickle of warmth swirled to form his head. It flowed downward to create his chest and limbs. He noticed his heart beating. Had it been beating the whole time?

Now he felt heavy, solid and real. He flexed his fingers and shook out his legs. Looking down he could see himself, normal and whole.

He breathed deeply. I did it!

A rumbling sound filled the cave. He turned to see the rock face rearranging itself to close the gap left by his body. His legs felt like jelly.

You have found me.

Adam frowned at Tya. *What did you say?*

I didn't say anything. She shrugged.

Someone else is here. Adam looked around. *Who are you? What do you want?* He sent the question silently into the cave.

The voice in Adam's head laughed. The gravelly sound had a mischievous, almost child-like quality. *The question is, what do you want?*

We want to get out of here! Adam turned in a circle, looking at the rock ceiling above, sending his thoughts to this other being. *Can you help?*

Again, the playful voice answered with a question. *The question is, can you help?*

Tya was watching him. *What's happening?*

Someone is trying to trick us. Can't you hear him?

Tya shook her head.

Adam pressed his lips together and then he smiled. He knew what was happening. It was a skull talking. Finally, this thing he could do might be useful and help them get out of there.

You think I am a skull? Hahahaaaa! I am crystal. I have knowledge, but I am not a skull! Look around, Son of Earth!

Adam approached Tya and touched the barrier. Tya did the same, matching her fingers to his. Even though the obstacle stood between them, Adam felt connected to her. Look around, he directed. *Do you see anything made of crystal? Not a skull.*

Something else.

Tya turned around. She stepped back and pointed. *There. In the middle of the lake. Do you see it?*

In the center of the lake something shimmered faintly in the half-light. Were there chunks of glass on the surface of the lake? Or a glass sculpture? The shaft of sunlight coming in from the gap in the roof shifted, and a shining crystal island appeared. At the top of the island, a crystal hand reached toward the sky.

Are you the hand on the island? Adam asked.

I look like a hand, but I am much more.

Can you help us get out of here?

My help you need.

Adam looked at Tya. *We need the hand. It can help us get out of here.*

Tya entered the water and swam with strong strokes to the island. Scrambling up the clear rocks to the top, she stood about ten feet above the water. Tya grabbed the life-sized crystal hand. It didn't move. She pulled harder and still nothing happened. She looked back at Adam.

Why can't Tya pick you up?

To retrieve me, together you must turn the key.

Adam relayed the information to Tya. *I don't know what it means,* he added.

Tya searched the base of the hand and found nothing. Adam watched her look around the small crystal island, walking in a downward spiral until she was almost at the water's edge. She crouched down and reached into a crevice.

Have you found something? Adam asked.

She stood up with something small in her hand. *It's a key. I'm going to try unlocking the statue.* Tya inserted the key back into the crevice and the hand rotated. As Tya scrambled up to the top, the hand switched back. Again, it wouldn't budge.

He said together, thought Adam. *You turn the key while I lift the hand with my energy.*

Tya turned the key and Adam tried to lift the hand. It still didn't move.

Why can't we move you? Adam asked the crystal statue.

Son of Earth can't move me.

Why did the crystal have to speak in cryptic riddles? *Can Tya move you?*

Daughter of Sea is able to retrieve me.

Tya, you lift the statue and I'll turn the key, he suggested.

She clambered to the top of the small island. Adam used his energy to turn the key. When Tya lifted the hand off its base, the crystal island dropped into the water and she disappeared below the surface with it.

Adam breathed a sigh of relief when he saw her come up again.

This is heavy. I can't swim with it, she thought.

Let me help. Adam lifted the statue from her with his energy. *I've got the hand. You can swim back.*

Adam moved the statue back toward the stony ledge Tya had crawled onto before. With an ear shattering crash the crystal hand slammed into the invisible wall. Adam jumped at the explosion and dropped the hand.

Scrambling out of the water, Tya caught it just before it smashed on the cave floor.

"Adam! You almost broke it!"

"It was an accident! I didn't mean to!"

They glared at each other and then Tya grinned. "I can hear you."

"Guess I broke the wall." He looked down at the crystal in Tya's hand. "Good catch."

"Why was the barrier there?" Tya asked. "And why did we land on different sides of it?"

The wall was my protection while waiting for the Daughter of Sea.

"The hand said the wall protected it while he was waiting for you," translated Adam. "This wouldn't have happened if we had landed on the beach."

The beach is near. You were both meant to be here.

"What is it saying?" Tya asked.

Adam told her. "It's nice to know it wasn't me who screwed up this time," he commented. "The crystal hijacked both of us.

This was meant to happen."

Tya traced the fingers of the hand with her forefinger. Something about the way she concentrated on the statue concerned Adam. "Are you okay?"

When Tya looked up her eyes had a faraway look in them. "I was thinking about my Nan. She believed everything happened for a reason. Wherever she is, I feel like she's smiling down on us." Tya let out a shaky breath and her eyes focused on Adam. "I know what this statue is. It holds the thirteenth skull, and their energies connect with the council so Atlantis can be moved to safety. We were meant to find this statue, but what do we do now?"

"Even though we will get in trouble, I think we need to talk to Noor about this," said Adam. "Let's go home."

Tya stared at him. "Did you just call Atlantis home?"

Adam blinked. "Yeah..." He smiled at the thought. "I think I did."

Tya's eyes danced as she reached for his hand.

Chapter Twenty-Two

Caileen carried the small, green skull down the covered passageway connecting the library to her father's office. She stopped for a moment to admire the beauty of the garden courtyard framed by the columned stone arches of the passage. A golden light danced as the breeze rustled the branches of the ornamental trees. The low rumble of Cavan's voice, heated in argument, seeped from his room. She hesitated at the door, her hand poised to knock.

"Who do you think you are, questioning me?" her father hissed. "I have everything under control here! The skull is your responsibility, Zador."

Caileen's skin prickled. What skull? And who was Zador? Her father sounded angry. Perhaps this wouldn't be a good time to interrupt.

Another voice spoke, a man's. "The archeologist has left Scotland." Caileen didn't recognize its owner. Why did he sound so far away?

"He must have found the skull and moved it." Cavan's response was low and intense. "You told me you were watching him."

"I don't know how..."

"Excuses will not help us."

"If the skull has been moved, why don't you know where it is?" the voice growled back.

Both men seemed furious. But...what skull? One from the library? One from the council? Or...the man had mentioned Scotland. Could they be talking about the thirteenth skull on

Earth?

"That is your problem, not mine. Find the skull, Zador, or you will end up with nothing." Caileen had never heard her soft-spoken father talk like this. A chill touched Caileen's neck. If it was the thirteenth skull they were talking about, the council and Atlantis needed that skull. And it was...lost?

"I'll find it," the distant voice snapped.

She knocked and opened the door. "I'm sorry to interrupt..."

Her father sat at his desk with his back to the door but jolted at her entrance.

There was no one else in the office.

He spun in his chair with his hand over his heart. "You startled me, my dear."

"I thought I heard you talking to someone." Caileen peered around the room.

"There is no one here. Just me mumbling to myself." The face smiling up at her was the one she had loved her whole life. Could she have imagined what she heard?

"What is that?" Caileen pointed to a baseball-sized gold crystal skull sitting in the middle of the desk, a faint glow fading showing the skull had been used recently.

"Ah, you have caught me. My memory is not what it used to be. I need to keep notes on everything. You probably heard me talking to the skull and getting mad at myself."

She had noticed him staring off into space a lot lately. He was getting older and the search for the lost library archives had been taking up a lot of his time. Perhaps that was what this was all about. "I brought you the green skull you asked for with the information on the Great Crystal. Do you need me to help you with anything?"

"No, no. I will be fine." He took the skull from her. "The research you are doing is very helpful. We will find the lost archives and the Great Crystal soon. There might be something in this volume I overlooked." Cavan stood up and took her hand, tucking it into the crook of his elbow. "Right now, though, let us go find some food. I am starving."

The gesture warmed Caileen's heart. He used to take her

hand when she was a small child, and he was planning an adventure her mother wouldn't approve of. "I'd love to."

As they left his office, Caileen looked at the man beside her. Her childhood playmate, her guide through early life lessons, the mentor in her love of research, and always, her loving father. How could he do anything wrong? How could he be the threatening, controlling man she'd just overheard? She shrugged inwardly, unable to explain it, but she'd figure it out. And then she could help him deal with whatever it was.

Chapter Twenty-Three

After lunch, Cavan returned to his office. Closing the door, he slid the latch into a slot on the door frame. No more interruptions. Taking a seat in his chair, his gaze wandered over the organized office. Shelves lining the walls held his sizable skull collection, and several more skulls were neatly arranged on his desk. The other members of council often joked about his love of collecting skulls.

His eyes came to rest on the gold skull in the middle of his desk. He stroked it thoughtfully, savoring the sense of tranquility he found in its presence. He'd stumbled upon the skull deep within the archives a long time ago. The skull had glowed when he touched it, and had said, "Find my twin."

Cavan hadn't understood the instructions at the time, but he found the skull intriguing, so he put it on a shelf in his office. From time to time he would search the library for the skull's twin, but he had never found the other skull. Many years later, the gold skull spoke again when the twin skull on Earth found it instead.

Whoever owned the matching skulls could talk to each other across dimensions. This was how he had met Simon Zador, Adrian Zador's father. Cavan's hands cradled the back of the skull. Noor, as well-meaning as he was, was not the leader Atlantis needed. Not now, with the black cloud threatening them, closer and closer every day. It was Noor's selfishness that had brought the cloud back after centuries of peace.

Cavan could think of no reason, other than Noor's personal desires, to explain why the cloud was growing now. It was clear the leader of Atlantis favored the Earth boy for his own reasons, and no doubt those reasons had something to do with Noor's trip to Earth years ago.

When Cavan had assumed leadership of the council during Noor's absence, he'd seen the potential: what Atlantis could be under a stronger leader. The Atlantis he controlled would rule in all the dimensions, just as he believed the Creators had intended before the problems on Earth had intervened.

And the small gold skull in his hands would help Cavan save Atlantis from Noor's bungling.

Chapter Twenty-Four

Noor sat at his desk staring out the window. He had seen the black cloud when he travelled with Adam. Now, less than a day later, it was observable beyond the rooftops of the city. Soon it would be visible from the city streets. A big black mass, rolling and billowing, a monster straining to swallow its prey.

Someone knocked sharply on his door. "Noor?" Raine called.

"Come in."

"What did you want to show us?" Raine hurried in, Alima right behind him.

Noor gestured to the view through the window.

Raine stopped short.

"The cloud is almost on top of Atlantis," Alima whispered.

Raine's head shook slowly from side to side. "It has moved more in the last day than it has in years."

"The cloud is growing too," Noor confirmed. "It will not be long before we cannot stop it."

Alima slumped into a chair. "If only we knew what was causing it." She looked helplessly at Noor.

"I noticed some changes in the cloud when Adam arrived, but I assumed it was because the prophecy had begun." A cold chill wrapped around Noor's body and he shivered. "But that does not explain the speed of its approach. Someone must be causing the dark energy to build."

Raine's voice was as tight as his expression. "Someone putting their own ambitions before the good of the community. Someone with the kind of command over energy that only we on the council possess." He looked from Alima to Noor. "The thirteen of us."

"Thirteen?" Alima frowned.

"The children have the potential to cause dark energy too." He pressed his lips into a straight line. "And with their training incomplete, their energy use can be unpredictable and out of control."

"And they are children, without the wisdom to put the needs of others first," Alima added.

Noor had to agree. "It is one of us. That is the only thing that could cause this much change in the cloud in so short a period of time."

"Then we must be prepared," Alima said. "It is time to bring the thirteenth skull home."

Placing his hands on the desk, Raine let out a long, slow breath. "I agree." He focused on Noor. "Do you want one of us to go with you?"

Noor nodded, reaching out with his mind to touch the thirteenth skull. Drumdyre...

Earth. Bones. A hole...

The skull was gone.

"Noor?" Alima sprang to her feet. "What is wrong? You just went pale."

Noor stared at Alima, his mind blank, casting frantically around the archeological site with his thoughts. He couldn't connect with the thirteenth skull.

"Noor!" Her hand tightened on his arm. "What is the matter?"

Raine straightened, worry and shock etching his face.

Noor took a deep breath and tried to quell the terror immobilizing his body. "I do not...know..." he swallowed, "where the skull is."

"What do you mean?" Raine threw his hands in the air. "That skull is connected to you."

"Noor, are you sure?" Alima asked.

He nodded. "It was at Drumdyre. Now there is nothing more than a hole in the earth where I left it." He could barely say the words. "Someone has taken it."

"You are exhausted. You need to rest," said Raine. "I will warn the council, and Alima can tell the children that we must meet. We have to decide what to do."

"Yes." The skull was gone. That was why he had been feeling so bone tired all day. "Yes. Arrange it. I...have to rest."

Raine and Alima left the room.

Noor's head dropped onto his arms folded on the desk. They had to find the thirteenth skull. Without it, he would die.

The wind blew Tya and Adam back down the tunnel to Atlantis. They clutched the crystal statue between them. Landing in the entrance to the Temple of Nethuns, Adam managed to stay on his feet. The thrill of the trip left a warm glow in his belly. He was born to travel.

Tya lost her balance and sat down hard, the crystal statue cradled in her arms. Tya carefully turned the statue over. "Whew. It didn't break. What a rough trip!"

Adam wondered why he and Tya hadn't landed in the library, the place they'd left from. Then he realized the hand had probably guided them. He hoped they could get to their rooms before anyone noticed they were missing. Though what they were going to do with the crystal, and how they were going to explain having it, Adam had no idea.

"When I travelled with Noor, we didn't go through a tunnel," said Adam. "Why was there a tunnel when I travelled with you?"

There were footsteps behind them. "Because you travelled outside Atlantis."

Alima? Adam spun to face her.

"What...have...you...done?" She fixed a steely glare on them.

"We were practicing..." Adam's mouth dried.

Alima's eyes narrowed.

"Honestly, that's all we were doing. Practicing and..." Adam grabbed the statue out of Tya's hands and shoved it at Alima. "We found this!"

"Come with me," she ordered. Alima marched them to Noor's office and opened the door without knocking.

Noor raised his head as Alima ushered Adam and Tya into the room. After closing the door, she thrust the crystal hand at him. "I do not know whether to be angry with them for being so reckless or surprised at what they did." Alima took a deep breath. "They travelled to Earth and brought that back." She indicated the statue.

Noor's shoulders relaxed a little. The crystal hand was in Atlantis. Maybe he would not die just yet.

He turned his attention to Adam and Tya. "Can one of you tell me what happened?"

"It was my idea to travel to Earth." Adam's words rushed together. "We were very careful. We didn't cause any problems."

"And how do you know that?" Noor would have raised his voice to them if he'd had the strength.

"No one saw us, honest." Adam's voice cracked. "And we were only there a short time."

"What you did..." he shook his head, "was completely irresponsible. How many times is this going to happen?"

"Travel from Atlantis to Earth can change the future on Earth." Alima's hands shook. "Not only could you two have been hurt, everyone in Atlantis would have been lost if you did not return."

"It is never to be done without a councillor's knowledge," Noor said in a stern voice. "Never! Do you understand?"

Adam nodded, his shoulders trembling.

Noor looked at Tya.

"Yes," she said in a small voice, tears flowing down her face.

Noor took a deep breath and steadied himself, leaning back in his chair. He held up the crystal. It wasn't the thirteenth skull, but it was connected to it. The drain on his energy lessened, a little.

"Now," he looked from one to the other, "can one of you tell me how you found this?"

Adam told the story. At the end he said, "We found the crystal by accident, really. I just wanted to go to a beach I know, and we ended up in the cave instead."

The crystal hand glowed and spoke out loud. *I was not lost, so I cannot be found.*

Noor looked down at the delicate work of art in his hand. "I think you have been brought here so the prophecy can be fulfilled. Is that why the children discovered you?"

Because of the prophecy, they found me, said the crystal. It paused for a moment and then continued in a booming voice that echoed around the room:

Three are needed for the power to be.
One from the sky and one from the sea,
and one from the earth will set us free.
For good or evil, unite the pieces three.

The hand went dark and sat in Noor's grip like an ordinary chunk of glass.

"Is that the prophecy everyone has been talking about?" Adam asked. "The one about me coming to Atlantis?"

"Yes." Noor cradled the crystal in his lap, and with a gentle voice, he became the teacher once again. "The prophecies guide us. The council's primary goal is to follow the prophecies and keep Atlantis safe from dark energy. You are the one from the earth spoken of in the prophecy."

"Okay, I think I get that part." Adam frowned. "But I don't understand what the hand and the skull have to do with the prophecy."

"The crystal hand joins with the thirteenth skull and amplifies its power, like the way your skull pendants work," said Alima. "When the two pieces are linked together and the three of you join the council, we will move Atlantis to safety."

Outside Noor's window, the sky went dark. A large crystal sitting on Noor's table glowed, sending a soft light over the room.

"Speaking of the council." Alima's gaze focused on Noor. "We have an important meeting when it is light out tomorrow. I am sorry for interrupting your rest."

"No. It was good that you did." Noor scrubbed his forehead with one hand and looked at the children watching him. Many things had changed since Adam arrived. Perhaps he had most of all. Still, it was his job to lead. "You are both wet and dirty. Go to your rooms, get cleaned up, and go to bed so you are rested for tomorrow. I believe everything is happening because it is meant to." Noor kept his voice was firm and sure, despite his misgivings.

Chapter Twenty-Five

Adam opened the door to his room. Orri lay sprawled on his unmade bed. His dirty tunics were spread all over the floor and a pile of his stinky popollama equipment sat in the corner.

"What're you doing here?" Orri frowned at him.

"It's my room, too." Adam opened the door to his wardrobe and grabbed some clean clothes. "Anyway, we both need to get some sleep. There's a meeting in the council chamber tomorrow."

"So, what's that got to do with me?" Orri stroked his skull pendant.

"Look." Adam threw the clothes on his bed. "Do you want to be part of the Three or not?"

"No! I don't." Orri jumped up. "The Three was just fine before you came here and messed it up. Play your little games with Tya, and I'll show up when the two of you need to be rescued." He stomped out of the room, slamming the heavy wooden door behind him.

Fine! Adam didn't need Orri's attitude or his help. He stripped his dirty clothes off and poured water into the basin. Orri was just looking for a fight, and Adam knew why.

Adam plunged a cloth into the water and washed the dirt from his face and body. It wasn't his fault he was the Son of Earth. Orri was acting like a spoiled baby. He dried off and got into the clean clothes.

Sitting on his bed, Adam punched his pillow and leaned back against it. Jeez, he was tired. Using his energy to travel, then get himself out of a rock wall, and help Tya free the crystal, was almost more than he could handle.

He stared at the blank stone wall above Orri's bed, still fuming at the older boy's outburst.

The surface of the wall darkened, an image of the black cloud appeared. As he watched it, the black mass changed. It rolled toward him, lunging and reaching out. Adam straightened. This was no dream. He was awake.

This was real. The black cloud was in his room and coming after him.

He had to stop it from hurting Atlantis! But how? Could he blast it with his energy? Maybe. He had to do something, so it was worth a try.

Adam leaped off the bed. He felt deep into his core to find his energy. It was weak, but still there. He pulled on the power.

He hoped this would work. All he had to do was concentrate.

The vibration flowed up into his chest, through his arms and out his outstretched hands in a bright flash of light. Yes!

The dark mass writhed as the beam of light struck it.

A black hole opened in the middle of the cloud,and sucked the light into it.

A cold murky wind wrapped around Adam. What was happening?

He screamed, but his cry was cut off. He reached inside himself for more energy, but his voice and all his strength were being wrenched from his body. The darkness swallowed him whole, and he became an empty shell.

It is your destiny, said a deep voice. *Fight the cloud.*

He had nothing left. *I can't.*

You can, the voice urged. *Believe you can.*

A hint of warmth flickered deep within Adam's body. The energy inside him was not quite dead. Concentrating on the small spark in the darkness, he forced every last drop of his waning power into the tiny ember.

His body shuddered with violent tremors. Gritting his teeth, he channelled his failing energy into his skull pendant hoping to boost its power. *I must stop it.* The thought sent a flare of white light flooding into the dark mass. The angry monster pulled back and roared, unable to extinguish the light attacking it. With an outraged howl, it retreated.

Adam collapsed on the stone floor.

Chapter Twenty-Six

"Adam, wake up!"

He opened one eye. He tried to speak, but he felt as if he were at the bottom of a deep well, swimming up through cold water.

"Why are you on the floor?" Alima gave his shoulder a gentle squeeze.

Adam looked from Alima to Orri and back again. Orri was standing there with a funny look on his face, like a deer in the headlights. Probably worried he would get blamed. Had he called the healer?

Adam wasn't saying anything with Orri there. "I'm not sure. I must have fallen asleep. I guess I rolled off the bed and hit my head or something."

"Does your head hurt?" Alima frowned at him.

Adam felt his head. "Nope, I'm okay."

"Did anything else happen?" Alima's eyes narrowed.

"Nothing I can explain." Adam looked at Alima, hoping she believed him.

"And you are sure?"

Adam glanced at Orri again, and then bobbed his head up and down.

"I see." Alima rubbed her chin. "Remember, there is a meeting in the morning." She turned to Orri. "And that means you too."

"Too?" Orri asked. "I'm the backup? The understudy?" He turned on his heel and left the room.

Alima frowned at Orri's retreating back. "I will deal with him later," she muttered to herself.

Adam crawled into his bed, facing his own wall, rather than

looking at the wall above Orri's bed. He didn't want another encounter with the black cloud. He also hoped to avoid Alima asking him more questions. Because if he told Alima what had happened she would tell Noor, and Adam had to figure out what was going on before he talked to his grandfather.

"Get some rest." Alima put out the light and left the room, closing the door behind her.

A hundred questions swirled in Adam's mind. Why had the cloud attacked him? Why wasn't it attacking Noor or the council? Why now? Why not when he had entered Atlantis? Did Orri have something to do with the cloud?

Maybe if he left Atlantis, the black cloud would go away. But that was what Orri wanted.

Adam pressed his lips together. What if his leaving didn't stop the black cloud, and Atlantis was destroyed? What would happen to Tya and the others? Blinking hard to clear the moisture building in his eyes, he didn't want to think about it.

What could he do, anyway? He couldn't save Atlantis by himself. A sickening lump formed in his stomach. What if he couldn't do anything? The biggest fail of all was doing nothing because it meant he didn't try. This was all happening too fast.

Everything you want is on the other side of fear. The voice was clear in his mind. The same voice that had spoken to him when he fought the black cloud. Then it had sounded like Noor, but now he wasn't sure.

He looked around, but no one was in the bedroom. *Who are you?* He asked the voice.

You will know the answer soon enough, the deep voice replied.

When will I know?

He heard no answer although he felt a little less queasy. Maybe tomorrow, after he'd rested, he'd be able to think more clearly.

The room faded, and Adam stood on a tree-shaded street lined with red brick buildings. It was a warm summer day. There were no cars on the street, and people walked down the middle of the road. Some were dressed in modern clothes and some wore old-fashioned clothing like the pilgrims used to wear.

People smiled at him as they passed. Was he dreaming? He shook himself, but the vision would not let go. It was like acting in a movie at the same time he was watching it.

He looked around. The buildings had signs on them. They were shop signs, and the sign closest to him said, 'The Broom Closet'.

So, you have found me. The voice was there in his mind again.

Will you tell me who you are now?

To hear me, you must feel me, and feel me you do, the deep voice replied in a playful tone.

The lyrical speech of the voice seemed unintentional, and the tone reminded Adam of the crystal hand. *You're the thirteenth skull.*

I am, the deep voice chuckled. *And you, Son of Earth, are connected to me. But you are not the only one who feels me.*

What does that mean? His mind filled with frustration. The skull was being difficult, and nothing was clear.

One step at a time, young Son of Earth. Because our connection is the strongest, it is your duty to bring me home. You cannot tell anyone about the connection we have. There is dark energy within Atlantis. There is one who wishes to betray the city. We must be careful.

The skull's words echoed in Adam's mind. Do this, do that. He had no choices.

Choices you have, but duties too. You choose how *you will do* what you must do. The voice of the skull was loud in his head. Now, all he had to do was convince Noor and the council he should retrieve the thirteenth skull.

Chapter Twenty-Seven

The stone walls rose at a 45-degree angle from the cropped grass of the empty popollama field. At the far end of the playing space, in the light of the glowing crystals circling the field, Caileen saw a solitary figure. Orri.

Her worries about her father had been interrupted earlier, when Raine had come to the library looking for Cavan. Raine asked about Orri, too, though Orri only visited the library to see her. Orri could be hard to find when he wanted to be, but Caileen wasn't surprised to find him here.

Not wearing any protective equipment, Orri bounced the heavy rubber ball used in the game off his hips, thighs, and shoulders, moving with an easy routine born of extensive practice, but with something else too. Anger or frustration.

It wasn't all right for him to ditch his responsibilities. People depended on the council to keep Atlantis safe, and Orri was supposed to be training to take his place on the council. Walking the length of the field she stopped in front of him. "Playing with all your friends?"

"Thanks." Orri snorted. "And I thought you liked me."

"Lately, you've been hard to like. What's going on?"

Orri gestured with his head toward the temple.

Caileen shook her head. "The kid showing up was prophesied, and I was never supposed to be part of the trio because my heritage is mixed."

"You don't understand." Orri let the ball fall to the ground with a thud. "Have you seen the way Noor looks at him? My father isn't on the council like yours. I have to prove I'm good enough." Orri kicked the ball, sending it flying down the field, then he scowled at Caileen. "Atlantis is my home. I want to be the one to save it."

"My father supports you too, so don't pull that 'poor Orri' act with me," said Caileen. "Like it or not, you're a part of the Three. You know how the prophecies work. You have no choice. Now that he is here, you *must* work with him."

Orri put his hands on his hips. "Why did you have to quit the training? We were a great team." His cheeks flushed and his gaze dropped to the ground. "You know what I mean."

"I do." She touched his arm. "But the training isn't right for me. The research I'm doing with my father is what I'm supposed to do."

Orri looked up. Caileen watched his eyes darken to a stormy grey as he rubbed his skull pendant. "Nothing will stop me from being what I'm supposed to be." His lip curled. "Not you, not Noor, and not Adam, Son of Earth."

Icy fingers of fear ran up Caileen's spine. Why was he acting like this? This wasn't the Orri she knew.

Her grip on his arm tightened, and she searched his face, looking for a clue to the cause of his outrage. Orri closed his eyes and let go of his pendant. When he opened them, the soft grey eyes looked back at her without a trace of anger.

"What just happened?" she stammered.

"Nothing." Orri shrugged. "The kid just bugs me, that's all."

"Orri, you scared me. You were so mad." She gazed into his eyes. "Promise me you won't do anything stupid because you're angry."

"Don't go all 'Noor' on me. I have everything under control." He tilted his head and grinned at her. "No matter what, just be my friend, okay?"

He wouldn't keep everything under control, and she'd forgive him like she always did. "All our lives we've been friends." The corner of her mouth lifted. "And that's not going to change, even if you're being a jerk."

"Thanks...I think."

"Anyway, Raine says there's a meeting in the council chamber tomorrow. You're supposed to be there," said Caileen.

"Yeah, I know." Orri sighed. "I'll be there."

Chapter Twenty-Eight

Noor had tossed and turned all night, unable to sleep. Now that it was morning, he was dead beat. He dropped his gaze to the granite floor just beyond his feet as he walked toward the council room.

Like all council members, Noor had a special connection to one skull. When the thirteen skulls and their owners joined together, they could move Atlantis. But Noor's link to the thirteenth skull was unique, it had lasted almost eleven thousand Earth years. Even though he didn't know where the skull was, he must still be connected to it or he would be dead.

Adam was thinking about his dream when he turned the corner to the council room and collided into someone.

Alima juggled the crystal hand and prevented it falling to the floor. "I would chastise you for not watching where you are going, but I was not watching either."

Warmth crept up Adam's face. "I'm sorry."

"What had you so deep in thought?" Her soft grey eyes, so different from Orri's, looked at him quizzically.

What had happened sounded crazy, but maybe it was time to tell Alima the story. "Something happened, and it could be important."

"What is it, Adam?"

He told her about his fight with the black cloud and his dream about the street with The Broom Closet sign but made no mention of his conversation with the thirteenth skull.

He shuffled his feet a little. "I don't know why, but I think the thirteenth skull may be in The Broom Closet."

"I had forgotten you are a dream channeller too." Alima cradled the crystal in one arm and placed her other hand on his shoulder.

Her fingers were much smaller than Noor's, but Adam felt the same energy flow into his body. In that moment, he trusted Alima. The feeling made him wonder if it was time to trust Noor again. "What if I can't do what I'm supposed to do?"

"We are guided by the prophecies." Alima stared up at him. "And I know it must feel as though you are being pushed into a corner."

Adam nodded.

"You always have a choice," she said, giving him a little shake. "And you must take a chance if you want anything in life to change." She smiled. "Do you understand?"

Adam nodded. He understood. If he believed he could get the thirteenth skull, they would too.

"Then let us go to the council. It is time for you to tell them what you know," she said.

When Adam and Alima arrived at the council room, everyone had already taken their seats, even Orri. Alima set the crystal hand in the center of the council table. Cavan and Vannen both gasped.

"How did that get here?" Cavan demanded. A deep vertical crease between his eyes made him look even grumpier than usual.

"Adam and Tya found it," answered Alima. "And Adam has something he would like to say."

All eyes turned to him.

Adam recounted his story about the black cloud once more. He finished by saying, "I would like to be the one to bring the thirteenth skull back to Atlantis." Adam's voice quivered a little more than he wanted it to. He took a steadying breath but Vannen spoke before he could continue.

"Are we sending the boy to Drumdyre to get the skull?" Vannen's slim body leaned forward.

Noor cleared his throat. "I do not think the skull is there."

"But you are connected to the skull." Rute's forehead furrowed and her red curls bounced. "You must know where it is."

"My connection is not as strong as it once was, and I do not know..." Noor shook his head.

"I know where it is," said Adam before Noor could finish. He knew it was a bad thing for Noor to admit to the entire council that he didn't know the location of the thirteenth skull.

"Earth Boy to the rescue," said Orri under his breath but loud enough for Adam and Tya to hear. Tya kicked Orri, making the older boy wince.

"And how would you know that?" Cavan's eyes narrowed at Adam in his signature 'bug man' look.

Adam stared back at him, determined not to be intimidated. "I had a dream..."

"Another convenient dream," Cavan mocked.

"Enough!" Noor scowled at Cavan. "Let the boy speak."

Cavan leaned back and continued to glare at Adam.

The crystal hand lit up. "So, you have been listening." Noor sounded relieved.

I am always listening.

All eyes turned to the crystal. Adam let out a breath he didn't know he had been holding. So, the hand can project its thoughts, even to those who don't hear skulls automatically. *Cool.*

"Do you know where the skull is located," Noor asked.

I know where many skulls are.

"The skull you hold. Where is it?" Noor asked, impatiently this time.

It is protected, perhaps from you.

"Is it protected from me?" Adam stepped closer.

From you? The hand made a grating sound that might pass for a chuckle. *No. Never from you, but you already know where it is.* The crystal went dark.

Cavan snorted but didn't say anything.

"Adam can you tell the council about your dream?" asked Alima.

Adam described the street and the sign above the door of the shop. "It was so real. Like I was there."

"I have an idea," Cavan clasped his hands on the table and fixed his mouth in what might pass for a smile. "I think Adam and Orri should go together to get the skull."

Voices filled the council room, everyone speaking at once.

Cavan stood and held up his hand for silence. The room slowly quieted. "Noor is old and not well. Besides, he should stay in Atlantis at such a critical time." Cavan spoke in a reasonable, pleasant voice. "Young Adam believes he knows where the skull is, but he is inexperienced and needs guidance. Orri is one of the Three, and he has more experience working with energy. He is the right choice to go with Adam." Cavan sat down, the twisted smile back on his face.

Adam looked around the table. Most of the council members nodded in agreement. A cold lump of fear sat in the pit of his stomach. The council couldn't agree with Cavan...

Orri might kill him.

"I can do this! I've travelled to Earth with Tya. We can do it again." Adam's heart pounded like would jump out of his chest and sweat beaded on his forehead.

"I want to go to Earth with Adam." Orri smiled at him and rubbed his skull pendant.

"I think it would be good for Adam and Orri to work together," Tya chimed in.

"I can do this. I know I can," Adam pleaded.

"I know you believe that is true," Noor said gently. "but in this case, I think two is better than one. And I think both of you should leave as soon as possible."

Adam watched everyone around the table glance at the opening in the ceiling of the chamber. No cloud was visible, but they all knew how close the dark energy had come.

"Good." said Raine. "Adam, do you have the stamina to go to Earth again?"

"Don't worry," Orri said. "if Earth Boy gets tired, I'll take care of him."

Raine gave Orri a look that shut him up, but Adam was sure that was not the end of it.

Adam was a prisoner, and the cell door had slammed shut on him. He was trapped without a choice, again. He swallowed hard to keep the rising panic at bay. What was he going to do now?

I will help you, Son of Earth.

Adam looked around the council table. None of the others reacted to the crystal's comment. Perhaps the hand had projected only to him. His heart rate slowed to a more reasonable pace. He would not let Orri have the last word. "I will do it with Orri."

"Alima, we need the location of the store called The Broom Closet," said Noor.

"I can find that," Alima replied. "Tya, would you like to come to the library with me?"

"Of course." Tya stood up.

"I need to check on something in my office. I will be back, shortly." Cavan nodded at Noor and then scurried out of the room.

"While we are waiting for Cavan, Alima and Tya to return, you two might want to get something to eat," said Noor.

Orri grinned and strode out of the chamber without waiting for Adam.

Adam wandered into the hallway and headed for his room, his stomach twisting. He felt so trapped. He needed to make this work, but he was not sure what to do about Orri. The thought of food was the furthest thing from his mind. *I hope the skull can help me.*

Chapter Twenty-Nine

Leaning on the railing of the small viewing gallery, Caileen looked down into the library. Spread out before her, as far as she could see, were stacks of shelves jammed with colourful skulls holding all the knowledge of Atlantis.

She breathed in, and the clean, fresh scent of the library overtook her senses. The world of knowledge waiting there for her to explore usually filled her with joy, but today there was something wrong in her world.

The library in Atlantis had existed for thousands of years and several years ago her father had discovered a series of vaults hidden deep beneath the lowest basements. Noor hadn't known these cellars existed, but when Cavan told him about them, he believed they might be ancient parts of the library forgotten over time.

The council had granted Cavan approval to research what was in the vaults, hoping he might find information about the whereabouts of the Great Crystal. Her father had asked her to help him. Because of that, she had special permission to use the restricted section of the library. Now she had learned that a skull that should contain information about a hidden vault was missing.

Taking the spiral staircase to the main level of the library, she headed to her father's office to tell him what she had discovered.

The door was closed but Caileen could hear voices. She knew she shouldn't eavesdrop again, but she couldn't help herself. She put her ear to the door.

"The thirteenth skull is in Salem, at a store called The Broom

Closet," Caileen heard her father say.

What was he doing? He couldn't be giving away information that might endanger Atlantis.

"How do you know?" the distant-sounding voice she had heard before asked.

"Because I have been paying attention," her father snapped. "Noor knows where the skull is. He is sending Adam and Orri to bring it back. Get it before they do."

"Lucky for you, I have contacts in Boston," the voice replied.

Boston was a city on Earth. The mysterious man was on Earth. Caileen's stomach tightened into knots.

"Orri is still under my influence, but it may be tricky for me to control him on Earth," commented Cavan.

"Don't worry. The skull will be ours," the voice said.

Orri? Under her father's influence? What did that mean?

"I will worry until the skull is in our possession, and we both have what we want," retorted Cavan. "I will govern Atlantis, and you will have the power you want."

It felt like a steel band had tightened around Caileen's chest. Her breath came in short gasps. What had happened to her father? Why was he doing this?

Unable to hear any more, she stumbled down the hall away from the office.

Back in the viewing gallery she slumped to the floor, slipped her feet between the railings and let her legs dangle over the edge.

The black cloud. The missing library skull. The spying. The thirteenth skull. It was a plan to rule Atlantis.

Her father wouldn't do those things. He couldn't. He loved Atlantis.

She stared, unseeing, over the shelves below her. Tension in her chest made her breathing shallow. The little girl inside her could not believe her father would do these things. Something or someone must be making him do it. A glimmer of hope flickered to life. The evil man on Earth must be forcing her father to act this way.

A deep breath eased the tightness in her ribs. She had to save him. She couldn't tell Noor. He and the council would make her father step down and vote to ban him from using his energy.

Looking past her feet, Caileen stared at the library below. She had to do this alone. But how?

The answer came to her. It was sitting right there, where she always found it. In the library.

Chapter Thirty

There was a bowl of pancha on Adam's night stand. *Who put that there?* He popped a piece of pancha into his mouth. As the hard seed melted, his mouth filled with the quiet crunch of salty potato crispiness. The potato chips reminded him of watching movies, picnics and birthday parties. He hoped what he was doing would help him find a way home.

The last morsel melted in Adam's mouth, and before worry could fill his head again, he heard the words, *believe you can.* This time he knew it was the skull talking to him, and because it sounded so much like Noor he could feel his grandfather standing beside him too. It was as if the three of them were joined: boy, old man, and skull.

Feeling the strength of the three of them united, he hurried back to the council room.

"Adam, wait up."

He turned and Caileen rushed toward him.

"I'm so glad I found you," she said. "I need to warn you about Orri."

"What do you mean?"

"I think someone is...well, making him think bad thoughts."

Adam laughed. "Orri can think bad thoughts all on his own. He doesn't need any help."

"You don't understand." Caileen's eyes glistened, as if she was about to cry. "I can't explain it."

Adam put his hands in his pockets and looked away. Why do girls always have to cry?

"Orri wants the same thing you do. Saving Atlantis is all he cares about." Caileen sniffed. "He...might want to do it without you."

"I know," said Adam.

"But someone is encouraging him to have those thoughts."

"Who?" Adam frowned at her.

"I can't tell you." Caileen pinched her lips together. "But I know Orri will help you if you let him think it's his idea."

"Sure, it's all about Orri." Adam shook his head and turned to walk away.

"No! Really," Caileen said. "Adam, I know you can do this. It's what is best for Atlantis."

Caileen looked so desperate. He shrugged. "Okay." Letting Orri take the credit might be one of the hardest things he ever did. "I'll try."

A smile broke through her sadness, and the tears spilled down her cheeks. "Thank you, Adam. You don't know how much this means."

He shrugged again. He didn't think such a little thing could mean so much to her. He started to leave.

Caileen grabbed his arm. "You won't tell anyone—about someone influencing Orri?"

Adam saw the worry on Caileen's face. More secrets he had to keep. When this was over the truth would come out, it had to, he couldn't keep all these secrets forever. He still was not sure he trusted her, but—"I won't tell anyone," he said.

Adam walked into the council room to find Alima and Tya hadn't returned from the library. He took a seat next to Orri and stared at the floor between his feet to avoid looking at the older boy. What was taking them so long? Adam squirmed in this chair and tapped his toe.

Alima and Tya returned.

Orri placed his hand on the skull, and Adam tuned into the skull without touching it.

Instantly, Adam's vision filled with a picture of the same street he'd visited in his waking dream. He would have no difficulty focusing on the location for the travel.

"It is time to begin." Noor's eyebrows lowered over his eyes giving him a very stern look. "Find the Broom Closet, go in, get the skull, and then find a secluded location from which to transport back. Do not take more than a few minutes and try not to talk to anyone. If you do talk to someone, do not tell them you come from Atlantis. You must avoid doing anything that might affect the future."

Right. How was he supposed to know what would affect the future?

"We can do it," said Orri with his eyes focused on Adam.

Orri wasn't angry, instead he appeared calm and confident. This Orri unsettled Adam as much as angry Orri.

"Adam," Noor said, "you saw the street in your vision. You take the lead visualizing the location. Orri, remember you might have more experience in using energy, but Earth is Adam's home. Many things will be strange and different to you. You are to follow his lead."

Orri nodded and held out his hand.

Adam scowled at Orri. He wasn't holding hands with him.

"Let's get this over with." Orri shoved his hand at Adam.

Adam clenched his jaw and rammed his hand into Orri's. He squeezed as hard as he could. The energy surged through them. It was so strong.

Adam carefully remembered the street he saw in his dream, and a deserted lane he'd seen between two buildings. He didn't want another travelling accident.

The council room winked out of existence, and they were thrust into darkness. A wind lifted them as they flew down the passageway toward Earth. Adam noticed this time the gale was steady and controlled.

The tunnel disappeared, and they were standing in a small, empty lane. Orri dropped his hand and quickly stepped away. Adam signalled for Orri to follow him. They crept to the end of the alley and stepped out onto a street shaded with large trees. A hot sun shone in a cloudless sky. An assortment of red brick buildings lined either side of the street. There were no cars, just people. This was the street he had seen in his dream.

As he looked around, he noticed that Orri wore a t-shirt and shorts instead of the tunic he usually had on in Atlantis. Adam had a similar outfit on. He shrugged. Whatever.

"Weird clothes," Orri commented, looking at everything like a tourist. He turned and stared in the sky. "What's that?"

Adam grabbed him and turned him around. "It's called the sun. Whatever you do, don't stare at it. It can hurt your eyes. Besides, it completely shows that you are not from this planet. Or any planet."

Orri said nothing, and he blinked as if he could see nothing but spots.

They had no time to gawk. On the corner, a large crowd stood on the red brick pavement. So much for not being seen.

"Come on." Winding his way through the mass of people to the front of the crowd, Adam led Orri to a ribbon of yellow police tape stretched across an open door. Above the door the painted sign said, "The Broom Closet". Inside the shop, uniformed police officers interviewed a couple of men in regular clothes.

Oh, great. They weren't supposed to spend more than five minutes here, and already there was a problem. Might as well break all the rules now. "What happened?" Adam asked the women standing next to him.

Orri glared at him and Adam scowled back. He knew he wasn't supposed to speak to anyone, but how was he going to find out what was happening.

"I think something was stolen from the store. It must have been valuable, to have so many cops here."

Would they consider a crystal skull valuable?

Before he could figure out what to do next, two men came out of the store. They stood in front of the crowd and the shorter man spoke in a loud voice. "I'm sorry, but the store will be closed today. Some of our artifacts have gone missing. The police are on the case and I'm sure the missing items will be found soon. Please come and visit us another day." As he finished speaking the man smiled at the crowd as if to confirm he believed what he said. The taller man beside him looked less convinced.

Something about the man seemed familiar to Adam. As the crowd moved away, Adam approached him, the feeling of familiarity giving him confidence. "Excuse me," he said, detaining the dark-haired man as the other went inside. "Can you tell us what's gone missing?"

Chapter Thirty-One

"It's an active police investigation so I can't give you any details," James told the young boy in front of him, as the crowd drifted away. Something about the boy's eyes made him think he knew him. That was crazy.

"Was a large crystal skull one of the things taken?"

James started. "Why would you ask that?" No one knew about the skull. Matthew had kept it in the back room, locked in a safe.

"We heard The Broom Closet recently got a crystal skull," the boy's friend said, and the first boy gave him a peculiar look. This second boy was taller and more muscular. They seemed like an odd match.

"What makes you say that," asked James. The feeling he knew this kid grew stronger. Here we go again with the strange thoughts. The skull was gone so he couldn't blame it for his weird ideas...could he?

"I know the skull needs to be protected," the shorter boy said. "We're here to help."

"How old are you, anyway?" The boy's information was too accurate. "And why would you think you can help?"

"I'm twelve," he announced, standing tall.

A memory of the baby boy he gave up for adoption after his wife died twelve years ago, flashed through James' mind.

✧✧✧

Adam watched a sad look pass across the man's face. What could it mean?

"You know the skull is special, don't you?" Orri's voice was low and confident. Orri had figured out he couldn't stare at everything like he was from Mars. And, evidently, they'd both agreed to break all the rules. Great.

The man paused and then nodded.

"I know we're just kids, but we came here to protect the skull." Orri's voice had a know-it-all tone like Tya's. Adam couldn't believe what he was hearing. Trust Orri to think he could convince an adult he knew what to do.

"This just keeps getting stranger and stranger." The man shook his head.

"I'm Orri and this is Adam," Orri said. "Can you tell us what happened?"

The man looked uncomfortable for a moment, then he shook his head again and spoke in a low voice. "All right. All I know is, at six o'clock this morning the alarm went off. The police received an automatic call, but by the time they got here, the thieves had fled with everything from the safe. The police are searching the town and the warehouses near the dock."

Go to the blue warehouse. The thought was unmistakable and strong in Adam's mind. "The blue warehouse!" he cried.

"What?" the man asked.

"Do you know where a blue warehouse is?" Adam insisted.

"Did you hear something?" Orri asked him under his breath.

"How did you know that?" James eyes narrowed.

"Sometimes we just get a hunch." Orri smiled and shrugged. "I can't explain it. You'll just have to trust us."

Wow, Orri believed him. Orri was supporting him.

"I don't know you." The man looked as if he would close the door in their faces.

"We know about the skull. And Adam, here," Orri clapped Adam's shoulder a little too hard, "has a hunch about the warehouse. We could be the bad guys." Orri smiled again. "Do we look like bad guys?"

"You have a point." The man laughed. "Okay. There's a blue warehouse near the docks. It's owned by a large international corporation that ships products all over the world. Thanks for the tip. I'll tell the police." He turned to go inside.

"Wait! The police have a lot of leads to follow up on," Adam said. "We can't waste any time. We don't want the thieves to escape."

"Can you tell us how to get to the warehouse?" Orri asked.

"Listen." The man looked over his shoulder, into the store. The police were busy with the owner. "Matthew doesn't need me. I can take you there. You've made me curious." The man led them to the back of the building. "By the way, you can call me James."

"I can't believe you pulled it off," Adam whispered to Orri as they followed James to his car.

"Sometimes you just have to sound like you know what you're talking about." Orri grinned.

Behind the store they all climbed into a white Ford Fusion and James drove off.

"Wow, this is great!" Orri leaned forward in his seat.

Adam realized Orri had never been in a car before, and he had to stop him from saying something stupid. Glancing at the older boy, he considered sending thoughts to Orri like he could with Tya, but now wasn't the time to test it. Adam checked the rear-view mirror to confirm James wasn't looking at them. He placed his finger to his lips and shook his head at Orri. "It's a nice car," Adam said. "My dad has one just like it."

"Yeah." Orri leaned forward and looked out the windshield.

They navigated through the tree lined, cobbled roads of downtown Salem, heading toward the harbor. A few minutes later, Adam saw several large warehouses ahead.

Good. You are close.

Orri gazed out the window, unaware of the voice.

Adam asked the skull, *where are you?* Then, he spotted the blue warehouse. "Turn here!"

James pulled into the gravel yard beside the warehouse.

"I'll look inside," said Adam. Before James could protest, he jumped out of the car and raced across the yard to a pile of crates beside a door. He clambered up and peered in a high window. The interior of the warehouse was dim. Two men sat at a table piled with money and crystals including what must be the thirteenth skull.

Be careful. They might see you, warned the skull. *The men are arguing about what to do with me.*

The big bald man thumped his fist on the table and said, "This is the craziest job we've ever done for Zador. I think he only wanted the big skull, but he told us to take it all."

"He doesn't collect stuff like this," the skinny man commented. "Why should we give him the other chunks of glass? They gotta be worth money." He leaned forward. "There's plenty o' money here an' he can afford to give us some of it."

"I got a bad feelin' 'bout this." The big man shook his head. "Let's just give him all the glass stuff like he said."

Adam had heard enough. *I have a plan,* he told the skull. *I'll be back in a couple of minutes.* He climbed down the pile of crates and, after checking over his shoulder to see if anyone had seen him, he hurried back to the car. "They're inside with the money and the crystals," Adam announced. If Orri could order everyone around, so could he. "James, can you go back to the road and warn the police? Orri and I will stay here and keep an eye on the thieves 'til you get back."

"I can use my cell phone here."

Orri gave Adam a questioning look.

"I'm afraid they'll come out and see the car," said Adam, doing his best imitation of Orri. "If you drive around the corner and make the call, they won't know we're here. We'll hide by the crates and watch the door to make sure they don't get away." He pulled the car door open on Orri's side.

"Okay," James frowned at Adam. "Don't do anything until I get back. Understand?"

Orri climbed out of the car, and James drove away.

"We're not just going to watch, are we?" said Orri. "What're you planning?"

"I'm going to do molecular transformation on the thirteenth skull."

"Are you crazy? I know what happened the last time you tried that. I'll get the skull," stated Orri.

Adam grabbed Orri's wrist. "Let's do it together."

"I want to get the skull." Orri's eyes narrowed. He pulled his hand away and reached up to stroke his skull pendant.

Adam clenched his jaw. No way was he going to let Orri order him around.

Then he remembered Caileen's advice. Let him think it's his idea. Adam sighed. "Okay, we'll do it your way."

The boys climbed up the stack of wooden pallets and peered in the window. The table with the skull sat in the middle of a small open area. Wooden pallets piled high with boxes and crates filled the rest of the warehouse.

"I can help by adding my energy to yours," said Adam.

"No." Orri's hand clasped his skull pendant.

"Whoa. I'm just trying to help." Adam put his palms up. "What's your problem?"

"I'll get the skull." Orri stared through the window holding onto his pendant. But the skull didn't disappear. Instead, it rose from the table.

Adam gasped. "You didn't do it right!"

"This'll work, too." Orri didn't look away from the skull.

The thieves saw the crystal moving and lunged after it. The skinny man managed to grasp the skull with both hands. "I got it," he yelled.

Orri yanked the skull out of his reach, but it wobbled wildly as he moved it toward the door.

Tell Orri to hold out his hands, the skull said to Adam.

"Hold out your hands!"

"What?"

"Just do it!" Adam pulled Orri's fist away from his chest.

"No, I've got it." Orri tightened his grip on his pendant.

The skull disappeared with a pop.

Adam elbowed Orri out of the way, and the skull dropped into his outstretched hands. His heart stopped as the heavy crystal slipped through his fingers.

Orri dove for the skull, and the wooden pallets they were standing on shifted. Losing his footing, Adam fell off the pile and landed on his back. Orri hit the ground beside him.

Adam rolled to his knees, and frantically searched the area around him. His throat constricted. "I can't find the skull," he cried.

"I've got it." Orri staggered to his feet with the crystal clutched against his chest. "Let's get out of here!"

James' car skidded to a stop outside the warehouse, followed by two police cars.

The two men burst through the door of the warehouse.

Adam and Orri jumped into the backseat of the car.

"There's not enough time to explain," Adam said, not giving James a chance to speak. "We need to leave. Just pretend you never saw us!"

James stared at Adam in the rear-view mirror.

Something about the man's gaze made Adam wonder if he knew James from somewhere else. Guess I'll never know, he thought as he turned to Orri, "You ready?"

Orri gripped Adam's hand.

The energy whipped between them. A blue glow spread from the skull, encasing them in a shining bubble. Adam's body was rocked by the sensations. He reached out to steady himself. There was no long tunnel, no path back to Atlantis. A deafening explosion shook the car.

Chapter Thirty-Two

The car crashed down in front of the steps leading to the Temple of Nethuns.

Steam belched out from under the hood, and its engine groaned to a halt. Silence filled the car as the three occupants stared out of the windows in disbelief.

"What have I done?" moaned Adam as he climbed out of the car. He pulled at his hair. "How am I going to fix this?"

Orri scrambled out of the car, still holding the skull.

"Not easily." Noor scowled down at them from the top of the steps. Raine and Alima stood either side of Noor, looking equally displeased. Tya stood beside Alima, her hands tightly clasped in front of her.

James unfolded himself from the front seat of the car. "Where..." He was pale, and for a moment, Adam thought he was going to faint.

"Hello, James." Noor's voice was cold and remote.

"Nathan!" Surprise of a different kind replaced the astonishment on the tall man's face. He looked around the cobbled streets, turning in a circle and shaking his head, until he faced Noor again.

What? How does James know Noor?

"It's been a long time." James' mouth twisted into a thin line as he looked up at Noor. "Where am I and what're you doing here?"

"Wait a minute, who's Nathan?" Alima frowned at James.

"He is." James pointed at Noor. "He was my father-in-law."

"Noor?" whispered Alima. The shock on her face rivalled

James'.

Adam looked at his grandfather and back at James. A heavy feeling settled in his stomach.

Tya chewed her lip and looked at him with wide eyes. Adam watched Orri frown at James and then turn his scowl toward him. Don't be mad at me, he thought. I don't know what's going on either.

The lines in Noor's cheeks seemed deeper than normal as he turned to Alima. "Some years ago, when I went to Earth, I fell in love with a woman. We had a child together." His voice trembled a little.

That child was his mother. Adam's eyes flew to James searching the man's face for any feature that looked familiar. No, he couldn't be his father.

"Oh, Noor!" Alima hands pressed against her cheeks.

"What's going on here?" James demanded in a loud voice.

"We will talk about it later," stated Noor. "I have to deal with this situation first."

A crowd had formed around the car. "I think this discussion should be finished inside," said Noor. He glanced up.

Adam's eyes followed Noor's gaze. Almost half of the sky was blotted out by a roiling, inky cloud. They were going to be too late.

Noor gestured at the vehicle. "Raine, can you move that?"

Raine scowled at Noor for a second, then nodded and descended the steps.

"Follow me," said Noor. He led them to Raine's lab. When they got there, the car sat in the middle of the lab, as if the room had expanded just enough for it to fit in amongst Raine's contraptions.

As they formed a circle around the car, Adam looked down at James' feet. Instead of the leather sandals everyone in Atlantis wore, he had on a pair of heavy boots. The scuffed brown toes and thick soles looked out of place. His eyes moved to his own sandal clad feet, standard Atlantis footwear. I fit in, but he does not belong here, he thought.

Taking the skull from Orri, Noor set it on a table.

"What's going on here?" James demanded in a loud voice.

"James, you are in Atlantis." Noor ran his fingers through his hair and sighed again. "Yes, Atlantis exists, but not in the way you think it does." Noor shook his head. "I do not know how you got here. It might be your connection to Adam or to the skull that caused it, but it does not matter right now. You must return to Earth. Immediately."

When Noor said the word connection, Adam's heart pounded in his chest. "I think I know what happened." His voice was barely above a whisper.

"Tell me," said Noor.

"There was so much going on after we got the skull. We jumped in the car so we could travel back to Atlantis without being seen." Adam gulped. "The energy was so strong. I reached out to steady myself, and I must have linked up with the car too."

Noor's eyes closed.

Adam knew he had blown it again. Every time, he screwed up!

Noor put a hand on his shoulder. "Adam, this is not your fault."

"It is!" He expected any second for Orri to agree with him, but Orri said nothing.

"No, I am the one to blame for what has happened and I must correct it." Noor cleared his throat. "James, our paths have never crossed easily and you have not understood many of the things I have done. So, you probably will not understand this either."

James folded his arms across his chest. "Why am I not surprised."

"Atlantis is my first concern, and I have to protect it above all else," Noor continued. "Atlantis exists in a different dimension than Earth. Travel between the dimensions can change the future on Earth. We need to reset the clock and return you to a place before the travel occurred. You will not remember your time here."

"You haven't explained my connection to the boy," said James.

Noor took a deep breath. "Adam is your son"

James examined Adam's face. His eyes widened and he

looked away blinking hard. "I never thought I'd say this, but I don't care about Atlantis." James looked at Adam. "I need to remember him."

Remember me? Why do you care now? Anger formed a tight knot in Adam's stomach. You're not my dad because you were never there.

"You will remember the events that took place before the moment we send you back to," Noor told James. "So, I imagine this day will stick in your mind for a long time."

"And...that's all I get? No explanation? Only five minutes with my son?" James' eyes were miserable as they stared at Adam.

Adam dropped his gaze to the floor, not wanting to see the sorrow in the man's face.

"I am sorry. Sometimes we have to put aside our personal wants for the sake of others."

There were a few seconds of heavy silence before Raine proudly announced the car had been fixed, and James could return to Earth. The glow of Raine's energy around the car faded quickly.

"It is time for you to go," said Noor.

"Can't I stay just a few minutes longer?" James gazed at Adam. "What difference would it make?"

"Travel between Atlantis and Earth is risky enough," Noor said. "But you travelled by accident from Earth's linear time to the fluid time of Atlantis, and that is very dangerous. We are risking your future. You must go. Now," Noor said with a finality that left no room for questions.

"I loved you so much." James reached out to Adam, but dropped his hand when Adam stepped away from him.

"It devastated me to let you go. But when your mother..." he stopped and choked on the words, "died, my entire world fell apart. I didn't know what to do with you. My life, such as it was, wasn't a place for a single father with a tiny baby.

"I've hated myself every day, and I wondered about you all the time. I would have done anything to get this moment with you. And now I have it." James indicated Noor. "He tells me that I won't remember it, and I don't have time to tell you how much I love you, how much you mean to me." Tears ran down his face as he spoke. "I hope you are happy with your life, and that the people who adopted you know how special you are."

Love me? Adam's throat tightened. He was a bundle of feelings, none of which he understood. He could see this man's heart was breaking, but he had nothing for him. "You gave me away. Just get out of here."

"James, leave now." Noor insisted, echoing Adam's words.

Reluctantly, James climbed into the car and started it.

The car flickered and disappeared.

On Earth, James' car skidded to a stop outside the warehouse, followed by two police cars. The two thieves ran out of the warehouse and immediately, a dozen cops surrounded them.

. Later, James answered the policemen honestly when he said he didn't have any idea where the two kids who helped him went.

Chapter Thirty-Three

Adam wiped his sleeve across his eyes and peered at Noor, his mentor and his grandfather. The pounding in his chest slowed a little. He examined the rough-hewn features of Noor's face. Noor was just a man who wanted an ordinary life.

Adam remembered his parents telling him his biological father had given him up because he wanted him to grow up in a normal family. He had always wondered what that meant, but now it made sense.

He had a normal family—a father, a mother and two sisters. Even if they didn't always understand him, they loved him and accepted him. He had what Noor didn't.

Noor wanted a family. I have a family on Earth, and I've found another one here. Inside Adam's tight chest a wave of understanding entered his heart. He smiled up at his grandfather.

"Do you forgive me?" Noor asked.

"Yeah," Adam answered.

"Thank you." Noor looked into Adam's green eyes that were a mirror of his own. He wondered if that was how forgiveness started. Not with fanfare but with pain slowly packing its things, until one day, it slipped away.

"I know you need to rest and I do, too," Noor rubbed his forehead. "But we have to finish what has been started."

"Let me help," Alima said to Noor. "I can give all of you an energy boost."

She moved to stand in front of Adam and reaching up she placed her hands on his shoulders. After a moment the boy beamed at her. She repeated her actions with Orri and smiled at Tya before moving to stand beside Noor.

"Go to the council room," Noor said to the three. "There will be pancha for you to eat, and everyone else will be there soon. I have to talk to Alima and Raine for a moment."

Noor watched the three kids leave the room, and then turned to Alima and Raine. What would I have done without my two friends, he wondered. How can I get them to forgive me?

"What you did caused the black cloud." Raine's voice shook and his hands clenched at his sides. "You say you love Atlantis and would do anything to keep her safe, then why would you do something like this?"

"It started out so innocently, and by the time I realised the fabric of time could be torn by my actions, it was too late." Noor bowed his head. "Since Adam's arrival I have discovered you are right about the black cloud. It is my fault."

Raine threw his hands up in the air. "Then why didn't you say something?"

"Raine, calm down," Alima's voice sounded like a parent scolding a child. She paused and breathed out before continuing in a softer voice. "Angry words are not helping the situation. Can't you see that Noor had no intention of hurting Atlantis? I do not believe he is at fault, because without his actions, young Adam would not be here to fulfill the prophecy. The Creators must have been using Noor to make the prophecy happen."

A warmth spread through Noor's chest. Trust Alima to see the good in a situation. "I had not thought of it that way." He smiled at her.

"I am still not convinced, but there is no use crying over broken glass." Raine cleared his throat. "It is time to fix this situation, no matter who caused it." He strode through the lab and out the door without looking back.

Alima smiled up at Noor and grasped both his hands with her much smaller ones. A soothing wave of energy flowed into him like a warm breeze on a summer day. "That will have to do for now," she said. "You will need a full healing session when this is over."

Noor nodded, unable to form the words to thank her for all she did for him.

"Let us go to the council room," said Alima.

Chapter Thirty-Four

"**Good. Now we** can get started," declared Raine as the entire council, including Tya, Orri and Adam, gathered around the council table. He set the crystal hand on a small round platform in front of Noor. Then Alima nestled the skull into the palm of the hand. The skull twisted back and forth like a small child wiggling to find a comfortable spot. It ceased moving and a soft blue radiance surrounded both crystals.

Raine looked at Noor.

Noor nodded and twelve skulls appeared around the table. They were as varied as the people sitting there. Some skulls were small, some were large, and some in-between. There were clear ones, pink, blue, and green ones.

Adam blinked when a teal coloured skull the size of a tennis ball popped up in front of him. Noor smiled. Adam reached out and touched the skull. The tentative touch became a caress, and energy from the skull flowed through his body. The connection was made.

Thirteen skulls sat around the table. A small spark of light glowed in each of them. The embers in the skulls grew, until a soft glow embraced the room.

All thirteen of the people linked hands. Adam took Tya and Alima's.

"I will be the lead visualizer of the city's destination," Noor said, closing his eyes. Adam squeezed his eyes shut and emptied his mind, surges of energy coursing through him from the others around the table.

No images came into Adam's brain, and his nose itched.

Someone across the table coughed.

Noor sighed, and Adam opened his eyes. Tya and Alima broke contact. Noor leaned forward and jiggled the skull. Adam heard a small click, like a key turning in a lock.

"Something must be wrong." Noor narrowed his eyes. "The skull and the hand fit together. The energy field should be complete, but the skull is not amplifying our energies." Silence filled the council room. No one offered any solutions.

What was going on?

Evil is here. You must protect me. The words popped into Adam's head.

He looked at Noor but Noor's face showed no sign he had heard the skull. Weird. *Why can't Noor hear you?*

The skull was silent. Adam's stomach sickened.

He tried another question. *Who is evil?*

Again, the skull was silent.

"Cavan, you created the hand. Do you know what is wrong?" Worry was clearly stamped on Noor's face.

Cavan showed no expression. "Perhaps the three of them," he said motioning toward Tya, Orri and Adam, "need to touch the skull."

The knot of worry in Adam's stomach grew. Noor's confusion and Cavan's calmness didn't make sense. What was happening?

"Come on. Let's try." Tya grabbed the boys' arms.

Noor stepped back, and the trio moved in. Three hands rested uneasily on the skull. The blue glow intensified for a moment before it dimmed again.

"Nothing's working!" Orri jerked his hand off the top of the skull. He reached up and rubbed his skull pendant. "What's the big deal, anyway? This won't change anything."

Adam noticed Orri looking at Cavan. Did a glimmer of a smile touch the man's lips?

"We must be missing something." Tya frowned at Orri and stepped away from the skull.

Orri threw his hands up. "I can't do this." He stalked out of the room.

Alima rose from her chair.

"Let him go," said Raine. "He is not of any help right now."

"He might need someone by him," Alima said. "He cares a lot more than he shows."

"Give him space," Raine counselled.

Adam's hand still rested on the skull. Maybe Orri was the problem. *Is evil still here?*

Evil is still here, was the reply.

So, it wasn't Orri. Caileen said someone was controlling Orri. *Can you tell me who it is?*

The light from the skull and the hand intensified for a moment, and Adam noticed a small slot between the base of the skull where it rested on the crystal hand. He leaned in for a better look.

"What do you see?" asked Noor.

"I'm not sure. There's a space where the skull meets the hand." He pointed. "Do you see it? Is there another piece that needs to go in the hole?"

"Hmmm..." Noor's nose almost touched it. "Could it be an imperfection in the sculpting? It is not very big." Noor stood up, his brow furrowed. "But that is an interesting idea. It makes sense there might be three crystals because there are three of you. But the council only voted to divide the energy between two pieces" He turned his gaze to Cavan. "Is there another piece?"

Cavan glanced at the dent. "It is nothing. If there is another piece, I know nothing about it.

"The prophecy is not clear about what three pieces are united." Noor shook his head and sat down.

Adam went back to his seat. Something wasn't right, but he couldn't put his finger on it.

"Noor, you should be able to solve this." Rute shook her head, her youthful face lined with worry. "I know you said your connection with the skull had weakened, but you must have some connection."

"I do not know if I will get an answer." Noor closed his eyes in concentration. His breathing slowed, and his complexion warmed.

He blew out a low breath and shook his head. The skull

perched in the crystal hand, silent and sullen.

"Can I try?" Adam asked Noor.

"The boy knows nothing," growled Cavan.

"What can it hurt?" said Noor. He turned to Adam and gestured for him to touch the skull.

Adam's hand rested on top of the skull again. It remained dark. His hand caressed the skull. *What are we missing?*

I cannot tell you. Adam looked around the table to confirm no one had heard the skull speak. Unless, of course, someone was very good at pretending.

Adam frowned. *Why?*

I could be overheard. There are those with greater skills than you.

Adam shook his head at Noor.

"I have no idea what to do." Noor's shoulders slumped.

Adam could see by the pale translucence of Noor's skin, that the old man was struggling.

"Let us all get some rest. I am sure we will have more ideas in the morning," said Alima with her eyes on Noor.

The earth rumbled, and the crystals in the room rocked, dust sifting down from the ceiling. The floor danced, and they all gripped the table. Would meeting in the morning be too late?

Muttering, the councillors exchanged glances, but they rose from their chairs. Falling into small groups, they found their way from the room.

Cavan, the last of the council to leave, looked at the skull. His thin lips curved up.

The hair on the back of Adam's neck lifted, as if a cold wind had blown in.

If the evil wasn't Orri, could it be Cavan? Adam had never liked Cavan. Something about him gave him the creeps. He decided to follow him.

Chapter Thirty-Five

Slinking down the hallway, Adam stayed far enough back so Cavan wouldn't see him. The librarian turned a corner, and Adam rushed up to peek around the edge.

A hand clamped on his wrist.

Adam twisted. The grip became painful.

Cavan's voice was dangerously quiet. "What are you doing, Son of Earth?"

Adam pulled harder. "Nothing." His voice squeaked at the end of the word.

A sound grated in Cavan's throat, sounding more like a rusty gate hinge than a laugh.

Adam couldn't feel his body. He glanced down. It was disintegrating. His molecules were spreading apart.

What's happening? His heartbeat thrashed in his ears—or what were once his ears.

Then all the microscopic pieces of Adam slammed together. He stood next to the railing on the roof, with Cavan standing beside him.

Adam glanced over the side. In the dark, the pavement below yawned, a terrible mouth waiting to devour him. Black spots danced before his eyes and he flailed out to grip the railing.

"You will never unite the Three," Cavan's face was so close he spat on Adam's cheek. "Because you do not know what the third piece is."

Adam tried to back away from the railing, but Cavan's fingers clamped on his wrist again. "What...why did you bring me here?"

"Orri told me you were afraid of heights."

Orri. Caileen said someone was controlling him. The clues fell into place. A sudden chill filled Adam's body. Cavan.

"I thought this might be a good place for you to hear a message," the evil librarian hissed. "A message you have been working very hard to ignore, until now."

Adam tried to swallow, but his throat was too dry. All he could do was stare into the eyes so close to his.

"You will leave the council. You will stop talking to the thirteenth skull. Stop searching for the key. Caileen will take your place, and you will not interfere when I expose Noor for having brought this evil upon us. I will lead the council to save Atlantis."

Expose Noor? Caileen on the council? But she said she had mixed heritage and didn't want to sit on the council.

"You will do these things, or you will find yourself molecularly transformed into so many pieces, no one will be able to put you back together." Cavan's eyes bored into his, as if he were waiting for Adam to visualize the penalty.

He knew he had to do what Cavan said, or die by what sounded like a terrifying death.

"Is that understood?" Cavan's grip on his wrists hardened painfully.

Adam nodded. Leave the council. Stop talking to the skull. Stop searching for the...the key?

"You have been very lucky, and I want to make sure your luck runs out."

"What key?"

Cavan looked away from Adam. His jaw clenched, and his eyes darted from side to side. "Just keep your nose clean."

Cavan had said something he didn't mean to. Can I make him talk? Adam imagined pulling the words out of Cavan's mouth.

Cavan pressed his lips together. "Keystone." The word slipped out between his tight lips. His eyes widened at the word.

Adam had power to control Cavan? A councillor? Tell me, his thoughts screamed at Cavan.

"Great Crystal," croaked Cavan. Then he roared like a beast in pain and the words became garbled.

Adam pushed again. Tell me more!

Quick as a snake striking, Cavan released his wrists and clamped his hands around Adam's throat.

A resounding crack thundered around them.

The roof pitched, and the two fell to their knees.

The surface of the flat roof rolled like waves on the ocean. The stones underneath their feet crumbled and disappeared to be replaced by a cloud of dust rising from the abyss.

Cavan scrambled backward, dragging Adam with him.

The chasm opened wider and a section of railing fell to the pavement below. Adam's legs dangled in mid-air, his fingers clutching Cavan's sleeves, his feet struggled to find a foot hold, and dust choked his nose and mouth.

Cavan hands tightened again on Adam's throat, and an evil smile widened his mouth.

Adam's body shook and sweat poured down his face. He couldn't draw a breath. Stars clouded his vision. He was dead if he didn't get out of there.

You can save yourself, the skull said.

"Stop!" Cavan bellowed above the din. He had heard the skull.

Adam's desperate thoughts dispersed and one thought remained. Escape.

And he knew how.

In his mind, Adam stood on the steps of the temple.

He dissolved his body.

The molecules of his form moved away from the roof. He was about to restore himself when the tiny pieces were yanked back.

He materialized to find himself back on the roof, his throat still in Cavan's grip.

Cavan's laugh grated against Adam's ears.

I have to do this! But how?

If he didn't look where he was going...

Maybe Cavan wouldn't be able to pull him back.

Stars clouded his vision again. It was now or never. The molecules of his body vibrated, and the rooftop disappeared.

Chapter Thirty-Six

When he pulled himself together, Adam was standing on the street beside the canal. His entire body shook, and he crumpled to the pavement.

A second wave of sweat broke out on Adam's brow, as the image of hanging from the roof ran in circles in his head. *I could have died.*

Cavan was the evil man planning to take control of Atlantis. His actions had caused the black cloud.

And...Orri was working with him. Being controlled by him, he corrected himself.

He had to stop Cavan. But how? He remembered a park Tya had told him about near the temple. It might be a quiet place to think. A place Cavan wouldn't look for him. He pulled himself to his feet and moved slowly down the road.

The cobbled roads were cracked and uneven from the quake. None of the structures had toppled, but people were coming out of buildings all around him, some looking dazed, others running purposely for help, or coming to the aid of others. A woman ran up to him, called him by name and asked what the council was doing to stop this madness. She ran on before he could think of an answer.

Hang on, was all he could think.

He must rest before he could try again. Adam contemplated the dark sky. The cloud, a deeper black, crouched overhead, covering three quarters of the heavens.

If the cloud reached the far horizon before the council could act, the city would be lost.

Adam walked with care until he saw trees circling a green space. Some trees had toppled over and he had to climb over them to get to the rutted grass. The soft sound of running water trickled into the air. In the middle of the small park stood a beautiful white marble fountain. The lower bowl of the fountain held three dolphins standing on their tails. With their noses, they supported a large chalice. A zigzag crack marred the side of the chalice, more evidence of the unsettled earth. Water poured from the crevice into the lower bowl.

Adam sat on the edge of the fountain and trailed his hand in the cool water. His feet rooted to the ground with no help from him. The sounds of people in the city faded into the distance. A soothing pulse of energy ran through his body, forcing the exhaustion out of his torso and into the hand dipped in the water. A strange strength and calmness replaced the fatigue.

He didn't have time to figure out what had just happened because the image of the skull resting in the crystal hand filled his brain. A troubled feeling nagged at him, like a dream he couldn't quite remember. He recalled the slot where the base of the skull and the hand met. He closed his eyes and concentrated on the memory, searching for clues.

A lush green field appeared in his mind's eye. Another vision, he thought. Beyond the field he saw more green terraces separated by stone walls. The surrounding mountains reached up to touch an azure blue sky. A glimmer of light appeared in the middle of the blue expanse. He knew this place. He had studied it in school. "So, you see me, Son of Earth," a voice echoed from above.

The blue light shifted into two eye sockets and a mouth. Adam recognized the thirteenth skull floating in the sky. "Machu Picchu? Why are you here?"

"To 'unite the pieces three', this is where you need to be. But beware, another is looking for the key. The three must be strong, to do what is needed. If the piece is lost, all may be defeated."

The keystone? "The keystone is in Machu Picchu?"

The vision of the skull softened as though it smiled and nodded.

"Why didn't you help me in the council chambers," asked Adam.

"There is evil in Atlantis."

"Yeah, I know. It's Cavan." Adam squinted up at the skull. "Why didn't you tell me?"

Cavan can hear my thoughts when we are in the same room. Now he is gone, I can explain what happened. Several decades ago the council became afraid I could be stolen by evil forces, and they would lose their ability to move Atlantis. Cavan carved the hand when the council voted to share the energy of the thirteenth skull with another crystal artifact. Dividing the energy would help protect the skull from evil forces, as both pieces were needed before the power could be used.

The skull went quiet for a moment. When he spoke again his voice was very soft. *Cavan has a vast amount of knowledge no one else has, because of his connection to the library. I did not know about the third piece until I was connected to the hand. I cannot explain how that happened, but that makes Cavan a formidable threat.*

"And you let me fight Cavan alone? He could have killed me!" Adam shook his head.

You proved you are stronger than you think you are. I told you to save yourself, and you did.

"Thanks a lot."

Adam, Son of Earth, the skull thundered. It sounded like his mother when he had sassed her. Knowing better than to speak again, Adam waited.

I cannot do what must be done. The three of you must do it. I helped when you placed your hand in the fountain. I gave you the strength to go on

The vision faded away and Adam was back in the park.

He thought about what the skull had said. Unite the pieces three meant the three of them, and that included Orri. Great. He knew Orri could be helpful when he wanted to. He'd seen that when they were on Earth, but he also knew Cavan could control Orri. He had to figure out a way to free Orri if they were going to make this work.

✧✧✧

A small crowd milled around in front of the temple steps. Tya and Orri stood at the top of the stairs doing what they could to answer questions. Adam pushed his way through just as Raine joined Tya and Orri.

Adam looked up at the dark sky. The black cloud was a darker blot in the blackness, but more, he felt its presence. It was a constant reminder of what they faced. A trickle of cold sweat ran down his back.

"Please!" Raine cried to the crowd. "Information has just arrived. We need to tell the councillors. Please go home and look after the people who are hurt. We will make an announcement in the morning."

The crowd dispersed, and Adam drew Tya and Orri into the temple behind the statue of Nethuns.

"We have to go to Machu Picchu," he whispered. He hadn't wanted to tell Orri, but he was one of the Three. Always threes.

Orri faced Adam and the corners of his mouth turned down. "And how would you know we have to go to Machu Picchu?"

"Because I had a vision," Adam hissed. "The thirteenth skull told me."

"Had a vision," Orri mocked in a singsong voice.

Ignoring Orri, Adam turned to Tya and said, "We should talk to Noor before we do anything."

"He's too exhausted to be disturbed," Tya said. "What about Raine or Alima? Or Cavan?"

"Not Cavan."

"Why?"

Adam glanced at Orri. "Long story."

"Maybe we don't need to disturb anyone on the council. Machu Picchu is a sacred place and Atlantis was once located there," said Tya. "We should be able to find it by focusing on the energy it sends out."

Adam couldn't believe what he was hearing. Tya was suggesting they break the rules. "We can't wait until morning." Adam gestured toward the destruction on the street. "You're okay with not having council approval?"

"I've been thinking about my Nan since we brought the hand back to Atlantis. Now, I understand why she risked her life for Atlantis. Sometimes you have to do what you think is right, even if you break the rules."

Some of the tension in Adam's shoulders slid away. "Thank you."

Tya smiled at him.

To cover up the warmth blooming in his cheeks, Adam said, "The skull will help us, too."

Orri lifted his chin. "You always think you're so special. Maybe the skull talks to me, too."

"Does it?" Adam looked at him, not believing what he said.

"I...I don't know... Sometimes I hear things." Orri's face flushed all the way to his hairline.

"What do you hear?"

Orri shuffled his feet and shoved his hands into his pockets. "I...I can't...explain it."

"Then don't." Adam shook his head. Orri was bluffing again.

"I know we have to save Atlantis, and then we'll be heroes," said Orri.

"We're not trying to be heroes. We all make mistakes," said Adam. "I brought that car back from Earth."

"And I almost lost the skull when we were trying to get it away from those men." Orri rubbed his skull pendant with his thumb and looked at his feet. "Sometimes stuff just...well, happens. And I'm not sure why." He gave the pendant one more rub before he let it go. Lifting his head, he fixed his gaze on Adam. "This time I'm not trying to be a jerk. Noor is in no shape to go anywhere." He gestured to the destruction around them. "We have to do this. Just the three of us."

"What are we waiting for?" Tya grabbed their hands.

Tya is agreeing with Orri? Maybe this could work.

Unite the pieces three. Adam heard the voice of the skull. *Okay, I get it.*

"Let's go," said Adam.

Chapter Thirty-Seven

Caileen's fingers trailed across the skulls in the children's section of the library, listening to snippets of stories from her childhood. Stories from a happier time, when her father was her hero. The memories weren't helping her heavy heart.

Her search in the library gave her answers to her questions, but not the answers she wanted. The black cloud could only be created by negative energy strong enough to threaten Atlantis. The current black cloud began to form about forty Earth years ago, during a brief time when her father guided the council in Noor's absence. Instead of confirming her father's innocence, she had found more evidence he might be at the bottom of the problems Atlantis faced.

Trying to work up the nerve to talk to Noor, Caileen wandered into the softly lit garden courtyard near her father's office. Even this quiet space showed damage from the quakes, with chunks of granite littering the grass.

The sound of her father's voice drew her toward his office. I've been sneaking around too much she thought, as a wave of guilt washed over her. But, I must do this. To protect Atlantis and my father. Or was it, to protect Atlantis *from* my father? She held her breath and peeked through the crack beside the door. Cavan's back was to the door, and his hands gripped the golden skull in the middle of his desk.

"You cannot stop me! I still have Orri in my control and he will get me the keystone you know nothing about," Cavan muttered. "Without the library skull I have hidden, no one knows how to save Atlantis."

Caileen gasped. Her father *hid* a skull from the councillors? How could that be in *anyone's* interest?

"Is someone there?" Cavan called out.

Fear gripped Caileen's chest, and she fled down the hall away from the office.

She had to stop him. She had no choice. She must find the courage to tell Noor.

Chapter Thirty-Eight

"Adam, you saw the thirteenth skull's vision of Machu Picchu. You take the lead on getting us there." Waves of Tya's energy poured through Adam's left hand into his body.

He grabbed Orri's hand and felt the other boy's force flow into him. Adding his energy to the other two, their united forces surged within his body. He looked at Tya and Orri clasping hands to complete the circle, and saw they felt it too. They were meant to be together. Together, they were powerful. Together, they could do anything Atlantis needed them to. Three elements burned into one fiery energy. Their three bodies shimmered and disappeared simultaneously.

There was no tunnel on this trip to Earth. One second they were in Atlantis, and the next they were standing in the green field of Adam's vision, still holding hands.

It was early morning, and the sun had just peeked over the tops of the mountains. In the pearly light, tourists in the distance were watching the sun rise, and so their arrival had gone unnoticed. Their clothes had changed, and they blended in.

Orri dropped their hands.

"Wow, look at this place." Tya let go of Adam's hand and turned slowly in a circle. She shaded her eyes and squinted at the sun.

"Where was the tunnel between Atlantis and Earth?" Adam asked.

Tya stopped turning and gazed at Adam with wide eyes. "Because instead of travelling down a tunnel, we stepped through a dimensional portal. Atlantis was once located in Machu Picchu, and there must still be a connection between the two places. I didn't know there was a portal here."

Adam shook his head at the amount of stuff stored in Tya's brain. He surveyed the ancient city from his dream. *Where do we need to go?*

Go to the building in front of you, the skull answered. It's usually lyrical voice was direct and impatient.

"Follow me!" Adam ran across the grass toward the ruin.

"How do you know which way to go?" questioned Orri.

"Because I hear the skull."

Tya raced after Adam, leaving Orri no choice but to follow.

All the buildings in Machu Picchu were made of the same weathered, grey rocks that were excavated from the surrounding mountains. Adam climbed a short flight of stairs and entered the building the skull directed him to. Its four walls had vacant openings that had once held windows and doors. The roof was long gone, and the floor was covered in short green grass.

Adam searched for the next clue. In the back corner, stairs headed underground. This must be where they needed to go.

At the bottom of the stairs, Adam created a ball of light in his palm, just as he had seen Noor do, and held it up, illuminating the area. The small room had a low stone ceiling, a stone floor and four stone walls, all made of smooth grey blocks. There was no door. No way to get out, except back up the stairs. This couldn't be right.

Tya stopped beside Adam, and Orri slid into both.

"So, this is where you're leading us?" asked Orri. "What's your skull saying now? Or are we going to walk through a wall?"

Can you tell us what to do now? Adam pleaded with the skull.

There was no answer.

"Why would the skull send us here?" Tya looked around.

"I don't know. It's a dead end." Adam sighed.

"Orri may be right." Tya turned to Adam. "I think we can move a wall using energy."

"Which wall?" Adam indicated the blank stones around him.

Tya walked to the wall beside the stairs. Her hands patted the surface, and her fingers probed the seams between the stones.

Finding nothing on that wall, she moved to the next one, working her way around the room. At the wall across from the stairs, she stopped and created a light of her own. "This one has carvings on it."

Adam brought his glowing orb closer to the surface of the wall. "They look like pictures. Or maybe some kind of ancient writing."

"This wall is different from the others, so I think this is the one we have to move," said Tya.

"It's Orri's idea. I say let him try." Adam signaled for Orri to step up.

"Sure," Orri swaggered to the wall and pushed his hands against it. The wall didn't move. He took a step back and leaned in harder, his face reddening with the effort. The wall remained in place.

"You're not moving the wall, Orri." Adam gloated.

"Like you can do any better."

Adam let his light float to the floor and placed his hands on the wall. He gathered his energy and pushed it through his skull pendant.

"Look." Tya pointed next to Adam. A pinpoint of bright red light shone in the middle of the wall.

Adam took his hands from the wall, and the beam disappeared. Putting his finger where the light had been he found a small hole. "Do we need a key like we did with the hand?"

"Maybe what's written on the wall is a clue." Tya squinted at the pictures.

"Like you can read it, Miss Know-It-All," said Orri.

"Stop it, Orri! Being a jerk doesn't help. That goes for you too, Adam. We need to work together here."

The two boys looked at each other.

Tya turned to Adam, "Got any ideas?"

Adam stared at the wall, absently rubbing his skull pendant.

"That's it!" Tya grabbed the small skull from Adam's grasp. With the chain still around his neck she yanked him closer to the wall. The skull pendant fit into the hole. A section of the wall shimmered and disappeared, revealing a door.

Adam beckoned his light ball into his hand and stepped through the opening. To his left, a narrow hall went about twenty feet before it turned. To his right was a matching narrow hall. Which way?

"The walls don't go all the way to the ceiling here," said Orri, the tallest of the three. Using energy, he easily made the leap to the top of the wall. A deafening rumble filled the air. The floor shuddered as the partition walls rose to the ceiling, knocking Orri down.

"Did you see anything?" Tya helped Orri to his feet.

"I'm okay. Thanks for asking." Orri dusted himself off. "It's a maze about the size of a popollama field, and there's a door on the other side."

"I heard somewhere the best way to solve a maze is to always make a right turn," said Tya.

"Like you know which way that is," Orri laughed.

"Just shut up!" Tya turned away and walked a few feet down the hallway, but not before Adam saw her trembling chin, and her eyes pooling with tears.

"You're not funny Orri, she can't help it." Adam walked toward Tya and said, "I think it's a great idea." He hoped his cheerful tone would make her feel better. "Come on. Let's try it." He turned to the right and the other two followed.

Adam and Tya's light globes cast eerie shadows on the walls.

"Hey Earth boy, try this." At the next turn, Orri created a light ball and set it a few inches above his head. When he took his hand away, the light stayed in place.

Adam copied Orri.

After three right turns in a row, they had to turn left. And at the corner after that, and the one after that.

At the third left turn, Adam thought he saw something out of the corner of his eye. Something moved, but when he turned his head he saw nothing.

"Great idea, Tya," said Orri at the fourth left turn.

Adam stopped and gestured for Tya and Orri to come close. "I think I saw the walls move," he whispered. "We're being forced to make left turns."

"Oh sure," Orri said in a loud voice.

"Keep your voice down. We don't know who is listening."

"Aren't you the suspicious one," muttered Orri.

"You go first, and at the next corner tell me what you see," challenged Adam.

They follow Orri as he trotted down the hallway and peeked around the corner.

"Well?" Adam gazed at Orri.

"Okay, so you might be right," said Orri. "Now what?"

"Shh, keep your voice down," Adam warned.

Do we need to talk out loud? Tya's voice popped into Adam's head.

What about Orri?

"Cut it out! How are you doing that?" Orri shook his head and covered his ears with his hands.

I think he hears us. Adam grinned. *Orri, send your thoughts out like you were talking to us.*

This is creepy. Orri's thought was loud and clear. *I don't want you two reading my mind. If you try, I'll hurt you.*

Projected thoughts are different from private thoughts, lectured Tya, her silent voice sounding exactly like her speaking voice. *And we don't want to know what goes on inside your head.*

Adam remembered the first time he and Tya used thought projection when they travelled to get the hand. *We can travel,* he projected to the others.

What? Tya asked.

Instead of walking through the maze we can travel through it, replied Adam. *Watch me,* he said as he disappeared. *I'm on the other side of the wall. Come on!*

I can do anything you can, Earth Boy, responded Orri.

Tya appeared beside Adam but only Orri's head materialized, poking out of the wall. *What the...*Orri jerked his head from side to side.

Orri, slow down. You need to do molecular transformation on yourself to get out of this, said Adam.

How would you know?

Because I've been trapped before like that, Adam replied.

Whatever! Orri closed his eyes. His head vanished with a popping sound, and all of him reappeared beside Tya, his rumpled clothing the only sign of his entrapment.

The door should be about five shusi that way. Orri pointed at the wall in front of them.

Sushi? Adam asked. *What's raw fish got to do with the maze?*

Thirteen shusi is the length of a popollama field. Orri frowned at Adam. *What are you talking about?*

Never mind.

We need to stick together, thought Tya, grabbing the boys' hands. *We could jump straight to the door, but maybe this way no one will get stuck in a wall. I don't want any more problems.*

Who are you calling a problem? Orri narrowed his eyes at Tya.

"Tya's right. We need to work together." As soon as the words were out of his mouth, the walls of the hallway moved toward them with a loud grinding noise.

"Let's go," he shouted. They travelled to the other side of the wall, and again the walls moved in to crush them.

Three more jumps, and they landed in front of a wooden door. Only the sound of their breathing could be heard.

The walls had stopped moving.

Adam studied the door. He didn't know what kind of wood it was, but the golden grain in the door swirled in unusual patterns. Two of the lines moved to form what looked like a frown and he saw, embedded in the door, the face of a sleeping woman.

She yawned. Her eyes slid open and, in a voice sounding like the wind rustling in the leaves, she said, "I have been waiting many centuries for you."

"What?" Tya peered at the face.

"Greetings, Child of Sea," the door answered.

"Interesting. She knows who you are," said Orri.

"Ever turbulent, Child of Sky."

"Wait a minute, what does that mean?"

"And you, the quiet one." The door interrupted Orri as she gazed at Adam. "You must be Child of Earth." Her breathy voice continued. "The three together can set me free. And I want to be free." The face twisted to one side as if it had been hit. She turned back to them with wide eyes. Her voice trailed off, and she closed her eyes for a moment. Her eyelids lifted sharply. "I am the guardian of this place, and you must pass through me to find what you came for."

The door had no handle or lock to open it. The guardian knew who they were...another puzzle to solve? Three together. That was it. "We have to work together."

Tya frowned at Adam. "How?"

Adam shrugged.

"Really, you two don't know?" A smug smile lifted the corners of Orri's mouth. "We have to combine our powers, like we did when we came here. We are the three elements: air, water and earth. Together we create the fourth element, fire." Orri grabbed Tya's hand. "Fire burns wood. The door is wood."

"We can't burn the door. We'll hurt her," Tya cried.

"Look!" Adam pointed at the face in the door. Her eyes had rolled back and her mouth opened and closed as if she gasped for air. "She's being hurt now. We have to do something."

Adam reached for Tya's other hand and grasped Orri's too. The circle was complete. This time Orri drew the power into his body. The strength of Orri's energy surprised Adam. When did that happen?

Orri dropped Adam's hand and turned toward the door. A burst of white light beamed from his skull pendant, striking the bottom of the door. The wood erupted into long tongues of blue flame.

Tya turned away, unable to look at the lady in the door.

Adam watched, entranced as the flames engulfed the wooden slab, covering the tortured face of the woman. After a couple of minutes, the wood crumbled into a pile of ashes and out of the smoke, a misshapen face emerged. It smiled.

Thank you. Adam heard the words in his head.

The crooked smile faded away, revealing an open doorway and a room filled with heaps of stuff, as if someone had thrown everything they didn't want into the space.

Piles of swords, bows and arrows, and pieces of armour

littered the floor. There were pottery urns in many sizes, some broken, some whole. Sprinkled on top, adding a luster to the scene, were gold cups and plates, mixed with pieces of gold and silver jewelry. Poking up through the piles were large broken pieces of the same grey stones used to build the underground rooms.

On top of one of these fragments, a small oval crystal caught Adam's eye. The deep red gem glowed in the low light.

It was the same size and shape as the indentation at the base of the skull.

You have found what you came for, announced the skull.

Why didn't you help us after you showed me the building? Was it a test we had to pass? Adam asked.

To complete the prophecy, you three *must unite the pieces three.*

Adam pointed at the red stone. "It's what we're looking for. It's the keystone."

"You don't know everything," Orri argued.

Before Adam could answer, they heard footsteps outside the doorway.

Chapter Thirty-Nine

Tya turned to stand beside Adam, facing the sound of the footsteps, and Orri sauntered over just before the red crystal went dark.

A tall man in a business suit ducked through the opening to enter the chamber. "Thank you for showing me the way here." He gazed around the space. "What have you done with my skull?"

Adam didn't know who the man was, but there was something familiar about him. Standing taller, hoping the man wouldn't notice the stone, Adam asked, "Who are you?"

"Why should I tell you?" He looked at Adam with a smirk.

"I'd like to know the name of the man who thinks I stole his skull." Adam's stomach tightened. He wasn't sure how long he could keep the bravado up. Tya leaned into him. Adam could feel her shoulder pressing into his upper arm.

"Fine. My name is Adrian Zador," the man said irritably. "And you did steal the skull from me." His eyes narrowed. "I want it back."

He ordered Big and Skinny to steal the skull in Salem. "There's no skull here." Adam lifted his chin. The man glared at him, and the queasiness in Adam's stomach rose.

Keeping his eye on the three, Zador wandered around the room, his shiny leather shoes gathering dust as he stepped over rubble and moved objects out of his way. He stopped and looked around the room, slipping his hand into his pocket.

An icy cold energy rolled off the man. A shiver crawled up Adam's spine, confirming the evil he sensed oozing from Zador. *He's dangerous.*

Tya nodded in agreement.

The man walked back toward the children. His eyes focused on the pedestal where the now lifeless red gem sat. He stopped in front of them.

Oh no! Adam grabbed Tya's hand and pulled her power into his body to create an energy shield in front of the stone.

Zador reached for the crystal and his hand hit the barrier.

Adam stretched toward Orri but he stepped away, rubbing his skull pendant. "Orri, come back," Adam hissed.

Orri clamped his hands over his ears.

"What are you guarding?" the man asked.

Protect the stone. I'll get Orri. Adam silently told Tya.

"Nothing in this room belongs to you," Tya said defiantly. She stood in front of the stone, using her body to screen the pedestal from view.

Adam pulled Orri's hand from his ear. "Come on! We have to help Tya."

Orri jerked away from him.

"That stone has power." Zador stepped to one side of Tya to look at it.

"Is that what you want? Power?" Tya challenged.

"Now, now, no need to be like that. We can all work together," he said in a soothing tone. "I want to use the stone to help the world. It can do so many good things. Be reasonable. There's enough power here for everyone. We can share."

Share! Who did he think he was kidding? Adam pulled at Orri's arm, but he yanked his sleeve out of Adam's grasp.

"What do you want to do with the stone?" Tya's voice shook, and Adam knew she was stalling for time.

Why was Orri choosing now to be so stubborn?

"With the energy of the stone I will be able to accomplish amazing things on Earth," Zador responded in a reasonable voice. "Let me borrow it for a little while."

"Finders, keepers," Adam shot back to draw the man's attention away from Tya.

"Wait a minute." Orri held up his hand. "What would it hurt to let him borrow the stone? If we got it back afterward."

"No! He hasn't answered my question," Tya said. "Why does he need the stone?"

The man turned to Orri and spoke in a syrupy voice, "The stone has power. Enough power to make both of us stronger. Don't you want to be stronger?"

Orri nodded like a puppet pulled by a string.

They were losing him. They had to unite the Three. But how?

You can do it! I know you can.

Adam glanced at Tya, grateful for her support.

The man feinted, testing Tya's reaction, but Tya kept her body and the energy shield between Zador and the stone. Her jaw clenched with the effort of keeping the protection in place.

Orri wasn't listening to him. His eyes stared blankly and his mouth was slack. His hand held his skull pendant. When Adam concentrated on Orri's pendant, he heard a gravelly voice. *The power can be yours! Think of what you can do!*

"Stop it! Stop talking," Orri yelled, snapping out of his trance. "I can't think! I'll do what I want to! I just can't stand all the talking!"

Adam heard the pendant speak. *I'm just trying to help you.*

Orri stopped again. His eyes were half closed, his face now peaceful.

The pendant had control of Orri, but someone had to tell the pendant what to do... and that was how Cavan was using Orri!

The man feinted again, then immediately made a grab for the stone. Tya managed to stay between them, her face red and her breath wheezing with the effort. Adam knew she couldn't maintain the energy shield by herself for much longer.

Adam touched Orri's hand, sending energy into his body.

Orri writhed as if he was in pain.

Adam clutched his hand hard but Orri pulled back, twisting his body to get away.

"Listen to me!" Adam's grip tightened. "We need you. We can't do this without you."

Orri shook his head, and his lip curled into a snarl. "You don't need me! You're the perfect boy, Noor's pet. Even when you screw up, you're still the hero. Well, you won't look good this time, Son of Earth. You don't know what I can do. Maybe it's me who doesn't need you!"

"Hurry! I can't keep this up!" Tya's whole body shook with the effort to keep the shield in place.

Maybe Orri was right. Maybe he couldn't do this. He was just a boy, trying to be normal. He didn't know how he got to be Son of Earth. He wasn't born in Atlantis. He wasn't special.

Snatching his hand away from Orri, Adam's head cleared. He saw the hatred on Orri's face as he clutched his pendant.

Orri's skull. It could control Adam when they touched.

"Adam! Please!" Tya panted.

Adam turned back to her as Zador's hand sent a beam of light toward the barrier. A vein pulsed on Tya's temple, her arms and legs spasmed with the strain of fighting the beam of light.

The businessman laughed, and Orri chuckled too.

In desperation, Adam grabbed the chain around Orri's neck with both of his hands. Jerking hard, he broke the chain, sending the small skull crashing into the wall.

You'll be sorry!

Orri stumbled a little before finding his balance and standing up straight. He gazed around as if seeing the room for the first time.

Adam grabbed Orri's shoulders. "Can you hear me?"

"What happened?"

"The skull I picked for you was bad. It tried to control you." Fumbling to grab Orri's hand, Adam channeled Orri's energy through his own skull pendant. "We need you. You are part of the Three...the three of us." Adam nodded at Tya.

"Let's go," cried Orri, and the boys rushed to help Tya as the barrier gave way. Tya grabbed Orri's hand and reached for Adam.

Something inside Adam froze. He couldn't move his body.

The energy sucked out of his being.

He had felt this before. When the black cloud had attacked him. If he dug for a flicker of energy, he'd be able to fight it. He had to do it. Concentrating with every fibre of his being, he reached deep inside himself.

He found...nothing.

Orri and Tya stared at him.

Tya tightened her grip on his limp hand.

Adam's legs turned to jelly, and he slumped to the ground. He struggled to lift heavy eyelids.

Zador reached for the stone.

Must. Stop. Him. From hurting anyone.

Adam crawled toward the evil business man.

He grabbed Zador's ankle. Maybe he could distract him long enough for Orri and Tya to get the stone and get out of here.

He yanked the man's leg and his world went black.

"The power is mine," Adam heard a triumphant Zador yell. "Nothing can stop me now!"

Chapter Forty

Adam opened his eyes. Orri and Tya stood over him. There was no one else in the vault.

Tya dropped to her knees. "Are you okay?"

Hoping Zador's shout had been a dream Adam croaked, "Did we save the stone?"

Tya shook her head. "No."

His fault. A heavy weight settled on Adam's chest. "If I had been able to fight the energy drain..."

"So that's what Zador was doing," interrupted Orri. "This isn't your fault, it's mine. If you hadn't come to rescue me, this wouldn't have happened."

"Really. If, if, if." Tya's voice got higher with each if. "And if I had been able to hold the shield," her voice quaked, and she swallowed hard. "We would have the stone." After taking a deep breath, Tya spoke in a voice more like her normal tone. "The point is, we are all in this together. 'Unite the Three,' remember? Well, it didn't work and we have to figure out what to do now."

"Help me up." Adam held his hand out. "And tell me what happened after I passed out."

"When you grabbed Zador, he nearly fell over." Orri grasped Adam's hand and pulled him to his feet. "It broke the connection he made with the stone. We got the barrier back up, but not fast enough. Zador linked with it again." Orri shoved his hands into his pockets and shook his head.

"He escaped," said Tya. "We couldn't stop him."

Orri looked at Adam. "I haven't been very nice to you since you got here and...I'm sorry. You'd think I'd know how to be part of a team from playing popollama, but I didn't really understand what it meant until today. You showed me how to be part of a team, win or lose. Thanks."

Orri? Just apologized? Adam taught him something? Was he still dreaming?

Adam looked at his friends, and his heart was full. They had an epic failure today. Maybe it was what they needed to learn—that each of them could fail. And after they failed, they could still work together.

Against all reason, Adam had come to Atlantis, and he had found two of the most unlikely friends. A know-it-all, and a bully. He was glad. "Today, the most important thing was that we tried," he said, imitating his soccer coach on Earth when they lost a game. "Each of us tried to do our best. It's not the win, it's the fight, and we didn't give up today."

Orri raised an eyebrow. "You're kidding, right?"

Adam shrugged and grinned through the heat rising on his face.

Tya laughed out loud.

Adam grabbed their hands. "Come on. We must tell Noor and the rest of the council what happened. Let's go home."

"Did he just call Atlantis home?" asked Orri.

"Yes, he did." Tya smiled.

Chapter Forty-One

Caileen swallowed the lump in her throat and placed her fist on the door to Noor's room, conscious of the early hour. Tapping lightly on the surface, she hoped Noor wouldn't hear her knock. She sighed when he called for her to enter.

"Come in. I was expecting you." Noor sat in an armchair, cradling a cup of tea. A bowl of pancha sat on the table beside him, but he looked too frail to eat, even pancha.

The lump in her throat rose again, making it hard to breathe. Noor gestured for her to sit down. A tremor rattled the crystals on his shelves. Tremors had been rocking Atlantis all night long.

She didn't know where to begin.

"I suspect what you have to tell me is very difficult," urged Noor in a gentle voice.

Caileen nodded.

"Does it have something to do with your father?"

Again, she nodded. How could she betray her father?

"I usually find it is best to start at the beginning."

Somehow the mentor's calm advice released the dam holding everything inside. The words tumbled out of her mouth. She had no idea what she said. Noor nodded occasionally, and she rushed on, telling all she knew about her father's plans.

Some time later, whether it was a short time or a longer one - Caileen didn't know - she ran out of words and the silence left her body hollow.

"I know how hard that was," Noor sympathized. "We will deal with this together." His twisted, wrinkled hand covered hers, and, even though he had little energy to spare, his warm clasp sent a healing wave into her body.

Drawing in a long breath, she gazed into his eyes.

She might be able to face the future.

The floor and walls rattled again.

"Help me to the council chambers," said Noor.

Chapter Forty-Two

The three of them landed in the doorway of the council room. Alima and Raine stood before them. Seated around the stone table were Noor, Caileen and most of the council. Cavan was the only one absent.

Adam was surprised to see chunks of stone littering the floor and the table. *Wow, the black cloud must be almost overhead.* He gazed around the room. It looked like they were expected.

Alima ushered them into their seats. She stood behind Tya and placed her hands on the girl's shoulders for a few moments. Tya turned and smiled at the healer. Alima repeated the process with Orri. When she stood behind Adam, he felt the soothing waves flow into him, even before her hands touched his shoulder. He hadn't realized how tired he was until he received the energy boost.

"That should help a little." Alima patted his shoulder.

"Before you say anything, this was my idea." Orri said. "I wanted to be the hero."

Tya joined Orri. "No, it was all of us."

"What are we going to do with the three of you?" Alima pressed her lips together.

"Let me explain." Adam leaned forward and told them everything: from his dream to Zador taking the keystone. "I think we needed the keystone for the hand and the thirteenth skull to work together." Before he could say they were sorry for not getting it, Cavan hurried in.

When the librarian saw Noor and the others, he stopped short.

Raine opened his mouth to speak, but Cavan put his palms up. "You do not understand."

"No?" Raine asked.

Cavan's gaze settled on Caileen whose eyes were red from crying. "I am sorry," he whispered.

A tear trickled down her cheek. "I overheard you. I told Noor."

"Tell us." Noor's voice was quiet and sad. "Everything."

A small quake rippled through the room and everyone reached out to steady themselves. The shaking subsided. Noor nodded at Cavan. "We do not have much time."

Cavan hung his head. "Adrian Zador contacted me to brag he had the keystone." His legs were shaking so much he seemed about to collapse.

Caileen helped him into her chair.

"I carved the keystone when I carved the hand. It is the piece linking the two crystals together. I kept it a secret from everyone so I was the only one with the power to unite the pieces."

Cavan must have been planning to take leadership of the council for a long time.

"Now Zador has it and I cannot stop him anymore," Cavan's voice was as shaky as his legs. "How are we...how can I...fix this?"

Noor cleared his throat. "There are some things I would like to explain first." He turned weakly in his chair to face everyone around the table. "I believe Cavan placed a skull pendant he controlled in the bowl of skulls at the pendant ceremony. Then he used the skull pendant for his own gain."

Cavan bowed his head again.

"The skull was given to Orri." Noor glanced at Orri. "It had the ability to send information to Cavan and messages from Cavan to its wearer."

"It was you?" Orri rose to take a step toward the librarian but Tya held him back. "All those thoughts in my head? I thought I was going crazy!"

Cavan's head snapped up. "You would not have listened, if you did not agree with them."

With a loud crack, the floor and walls convulsed. A dozen crystals fell to the floor and shattered, and the light in the room dimmed. A shower of dust and debris landed on everyone, and the councillors cast fearful glances at the ceiling. The tremor subsided.

"Enough!" Noor's stormy eyes focused on Cavan, bringing the group back to the topic. "You will not blame Orri."

Cavan's shoulders curled in as he clasped his hands in front of his chest.

Noor shook his head and sighed. "When did all this start?"

"You went to Earth and left Atlantis unprotected." Cavan lifted his chin. "I did what needed to be done."

"I spent longer on Earth than I should have, and it caused many problems." Noor's eyes focused on Cavan. "It still doesn't explain why you did it."

"All I have ever wanted is to protect Atlantis. Surely you can understand that?" Cavan stared back at Noor.

Noor tipped his head in agreement.

"I do not know exactly how it happened." Cavan's eyes dropped to the table. "Somehow, I...lost sight of that, I lost control."

Lost control. Cavan wasn't as strong as he thought. He'd shown weakness when they were on the rooftop and he had managed to pull the words out of Cavan's mouth. The words. They were clues. Keystone, and...what was the other word? "What does the Great Crystal have to do with all this?" Adam blurted out.

Noor frowned at him. "Where did you hear that?"

"From him." He pointed at Cavan.

Noor turned to the librarian. "Have you found it?"

"Impossible." Raine stood and leaned on the table. "The Great Crystal disappeared when Atlantis was destroyed, eleven thousand years ago."

"It is still here." Cavan's voice was strong and sure.

"I do not believe that." Raine spat back. "We would have found it by now."

"Just covering up his mistakes." Thuan frowned and crossed his arms over his big chest.

Noor frowned at Raine and Thuan. "We do not need negative

comments at this point in time. Let Cavan speak."

"Where is it?" Adam prompted the librarian.

"I was researching the lost vaults, when I found some information suggesting the Great Crystal was in one of them." He scowled at Raine. "Whenever we move Atlantis, artifacts get misplaced. I believe those items are not lost but hidden somewhere underneath the library."

"I agree with Cavan about the lost vaults." Noor gazed around the table making sure no one questioned his statement. "And I agreed to him looking for them." The old man's eyes met Cavan's. "And despite all he has done, I think he loves Atlantis as much as any of us."

Cavan stared at Noor and swallowed hard.

Adam couldn't believe what he was hearing. Cavan had tricked Orri and almost killed him. Is Noor crazy?

"We have all made mistakes we regret," Noor continued. "But I think the most important thing right now, is the safety of our beloved city."

"Thank you. You are a better man than I am." Cavan's voice wavered. "I know what I have done was wrong, I can see that now. Because the keystone has been taken, we cannot unite the three pieces and move Atlantis to safety." He dropped his face into his hand and his shoulders shook.

"We will find another way to protect Atlantis," said Noor.

Alima walked over to Cavan and rubbed his back. "It is said we can use the Great Crystal to do that. Can you tell us what you have found?"

Cavan lifted his head and swiped his hand across his face. "I discovered a skull with some information about the hidden vaults. It led me to a room I cannot open but I think it is where the Great Crystal is." Cavan looked at Noor. "I know I will be punished for what I have done, but can I show you what I have found?"

Chapter Forty-Three

The council, including Caileen, adjourned to the library. Noor leaning on Raine's arm led the way. The halls of the temple were littered with blocks of stone, and the floors were fractured with cracks, making their passage slower than normal.

Once inside the library, Cavan guided them between the rows of skulls for what Adam thought was a long time. Finally, they stopped in front of a tall stack of shelves up against a wall. It looked like a dead end.

Reaching between two skulls, Cavan pushed on a brick. The wall swung silently open, revealing a granite staircase leading down into darkness. Crystal sconces lit up as Cavan stepped on the first step. The staircase spiraled downward and ended in a small room with no exit. All fourteen people crowded into the small space.

This is like Machu Picchu.

Tya and Orri nodded in agreement with Adam.

Cavan set the skull in a niche in the wall. With the sound of stone rubbing against stone, a big panel moved to one side. Behind it was another stone wall with the outline of a large left hand on it.

Noor held his palm up. "That might fit me." He placed his gnarled hand onto the shoulder-height silhouette. It was a perfect fit. The wall didn't move. Stepping back, he stroked a forefinger under his chin and frowned.

"Did you see this?" Tya pointed at the wall where three smaller left handprints had appeared beside the larger one. All three hands were different sizes, and at different heights.

"Hey, Earth Boy, watch me." Orri placed his left palm on the largest and highest outline. His eyes widened when it was an exact match for his hand.

Adam placed his palm on the outline beside Orri. Some unknown carver thousands of years ago had etched the perfect silhouette of his hand. This was so strange. How was this linked to the prophecy?

Tya stood beside Adam and placed her palm on the wall. Again, the carving fit.

Adam reached out and touched Tya's shoulder. When Orri did the same thing to Adam their energies melded. The feeling of oneness engulfed Adam. The lines of the carvings lit up but nothing happened.

Noor put his hand back on the wall and touched Orri's shoulder. Still nothing happened.

Alima stepped forward pulling Raine with her. She put her hand on Noor's back and Raine touched her.

With their strength boosting Noor's, energy flowed through the younger trio in a warm wave, wisdom and power blending seamlessly with youthful energy. Noor, Alima and Raine became a part of them, linking old and new.

Wow, this was amazing. Adam now totally understood why he had been brought to Atlantis. Together they could keep Atlantis safe. Past, present and future united, and their energy was fierce and strong. *No matter what, we are connected.*

Forever, Tya silently agreed.

Yup. Adam could hear the smile in Orri's voice.

The wall vanished without a sound. Before them was an oval room with a white, eight-sided crystal column standing at its center. The crystal was at least ten feet tall, and three feet across. The room rose far above the top of the crystal to a domed ceiling. Light radiated from the crystal, and reflected off the walls with a soft glow.

Adam touched the smooth white wall. It felt like plastic. Why would Atlantis have a plastic room? He looked around. The chamber was like something out of a spaceship. Someone thousands of years ago had carved the outlines of their hands and created this. "Who built this room?"

"There are many things we do not know about our forbearers," answered Noor. "What we do know about them is in the prophecies they left to guide us."

"Don't you want to know more?" Adam asked still not understanding why Noor and the council accepted the prophecies so easily.

"It is not for us to question. We do what we are instructed to do." Noor chuckled. "And so should you, young Son of Earth."

Adam shook his head. He didn't think he'd changed that much.

Noor's eyes settled on Cavan. "Thank you. You achieved something good today by revealing the location of the Great Crystal." The wrinkles around Noor's eyes deepened and Adam saw a great sadness reflected on his face.

"But it does not erase all the harm you have caused," Raine said.

Noor silently watched Cavan for a couple of moments, and a red flush crept across Cavan's cheeks.

Noor turned to everyone else. "If you agree, Cavan's talents will be suspended."

The skull pendants of the remaining council members all lit up.

Adam could see the pain on Caileen's face.

Cavan looked at her. "Caileen, I did not want to hurt you..."

"I don't want to hear it," Caileen interrupted him. "Not today."

Cavan's shoulders slumped, and his head hung down.

"Adam, Orri and Tya," Noor said, "your energy is not needed for this."

The three stood back as the council formed a circle around Cavan. They linked hands, and all focused their energy on the librarian.

A silence filled the softly lit room, and Cavan trembled for a moment, arched his back, and then slumped to his knees. The chain on his pendant snapped, and the tiny skull clattered on the floor. The room seemed to lighten then, and it smelled like the air after a spring rain. Adam felt as if a weight had been lifted from his shoulders.

The councillors released their hands.

The former librarian pushed himself up, and somehow Adam could not imagine the bug man look ever coming to this new face. He seemed happier.

"Cavan, you will spend the rest of your days caring for the gardens in Atlantis," Noor said. "I hope you find some peace there."

Cavan nodded and left the chamber. His power was gone.

When the door closed, Noor walked over to a panel on the wall beside the crystal. He tapped on several symbols on its surface, and a window on the ceiling opened.

The cloud covered the opening, blotting out the sky. Flickers of lightning lit the cloud with a dull purple glow, and thunder echoed around the chamber.

"It is time," said Noor. "The dark cloud must be destroyed so it will no longer be a threat to Atlantis. Let us finish what you came to do, Son of Earth."

Noor took Alima's hand, and she reached for Raine's hand. Around the circle each council member connected with the person next to them. Orri held Tya's hand. Adam stood between Tya and Caileen connecting with them. Caileen completed the circle when she grasped Noor's hand.

The floor bucked, and Caileen let go of Adam's hand as they all struggled to keep their balance.

A lump sat in the pit of Adam's stomach. Were they too late to save Atlantis? He looked around the circle and all the faces appeared focused and calm. He reached for both girl's hands again.

When the circle was linked once more, Adam felt the energy flow toward the leader of the council, and Noor channeled it into the Great Crystal.

They all stood very quietly holding hands, the thirteen of them gathered in a circle. The glow in the room radiated softly at first, then the intensity increased.

More energy. More! The thought came from nowhere and everywhere.

Adam reached into his being and brought forth all he could. It felt like a river flooding inside him, with power enough to take anything in its path.

The powerful blast of their combined energies surged out of the circle and into the crystal. The crystal brightened. The clouds above split and crashed, and the smell of sulfur and ash filled the air.

More!

The crystal vibrated, and the chamber filled with light.

Adam squinted against the brightness.

Rainbows shone within the Great Crystal. Rays of light radiated from all the skull pendants, filling the chamber until the room shimmered.

An intense beam shot up from the crystal column through the opening in the roof.

The sky lightened. Slowly at first, and then with a sudden swiftness, the clouds parted and thinned. Blue sky appeared above.

The cloud of dark energy was gone.

Banished forever?

No, not gone. The voice was not Noor's, but the common thoughts of all. *Banished for now and gone until the council can find a permanent solution.*

Alima sank to her knees. Raine bent over with his hands on his thighs. Adam's body was a hollow shell, and even Orri leaned against a wall. Caileen looked pale, as if she would faint, but she smiled. Tya touched Noor's elbow.

A ray of light from the crystal streamed down over their heads. A glow warmed Adam from the inside. What had been drained now flowed back into him.

Noor stood straighter than he had in days. "For eleven thousand years, we thought this crystal was lost to us." He smiled, his face illuminated by the fading light of the crystal. "I do not know who saved it or how they did it, but I am glad Cavan found it."

The others nodded in agreement, then laughed and dusted themselves off. The floor was still. The tremors gone.

Orri grinned and gave Adam a high five. Where had he learned that?

Tya came over and wrapped her arms around the two of them. Adam hugged her back, and somehow, he didn't mind it.

Noor tapped on the panel. The roof closed and the light in the room returned to a soft glow. "Atlantis will be safe until we can get the keystone back."

The keystone. Their work was not done yet.

Chapter Forty-Four

With Noor in the lead, the group trooped back through the temple to the council chamber.

Adam lagged at the back of the line. He needed some time to sort out the thoughts tumbling through his mind.

Adam watched Tya and Orri walking in front of him. He wasn't alone. He had friends who understood him. They'd showed him who he was, and what he could do. He wasn't weird. A warmth crept into his chest.

He had a family he knew nothing about. A grandfather. Someone who understood who he really was. The warmth hugged him.

They had saved Atlantis. Maybe not like they had planned to, but they had done it. For now.

Adam stopped as everyone turned the corner ahead of him. This was where he belonged. His stomach tightened as a wave of homesickness washed through him. The warmth he felt evaporated, he knew Atlantis wasn't his real home. He couldn't stay here. What would happen when he left? He might never see Atlantis again.

"Adam! Hurry up!" Tya stood at the corner and frowned in puzzlement. "What are you doing?"

Adam stared at her and shook his head.

She walked toward him. "Are you alright?"

"What will happen next?"

"The prophecies will guide us, and the council will tell us what to do. Just like they always have."

Adam stared at the cracked floor. He knew he had to go

home, but somewhere in the back of his mind a part of him wanted to stay and finish what he'd started. He shoved his hands in his pockets. "What will happen to me?"

"Whatever is supposed to happen, Silly." Tya grabbed his hand. "Come on."

It wasn't that easy. Was it? Maybe Noor and Tya were right. He shouldn't question everything. Maybe he could be a little more accepting. He still didn't like not having a choice. That would never change. He allowed Tya to drag him to the council chamber.

Councillors were righting chairs and getting seated when they entered the room and took their places.

Noor looked around the table. His gaze stopped at Orri and he smiled. "We need to find you a skull pendant."

Alima entered the chamber and placed the golden bowl filled with miniature skulls in front of Orri.

Orri gestured at Adam.

"Oh, no." Adam laughed. "I did a bad job last time. Pick your own skull."

Orri stood and put his hand into the bowl. A white skull glowed. He carefully lifted it out of the bowl and the skull's radiance deepened. "This feels right." Orri gazed at the small skull nestled in his palm.

Noor picked up the small crystal and with a turn of his hand it dangled from a silver chain. Placing the chain around Orri's neck he gestured for him to be seated.

"Next, we require another person on the council." Noor fondly regarded Caileen. "I would like to suggest we train Caileen to replace Cavan. She knows a lot about our library, and I think she would make a valuable addition to the council." Noor turned his gaze to the rest of them gathered at the table. He smiled when he saw all the skull pendants were lit up in favour of his idea.

"Will you agree to be trained, so you may take your father's place?"

Caileen nodded, her eyes full of tears.

Alima set the bowl of small skulls in front of Caileen. A mottled green and blue one lit up for her, and Noor put a chain on it.

Noor stroked the thirteenth skull cradled in the crystal hand on the table in front of him. "Now we require the rest of the council's skulls." As soon as he finished speaking, skulls materialized on the council table. Again, they were as varied as the people around the table.

Adam stroked his teal blue skull. The energy from it flowed through his body, and the connection happened just like last time.

"Adam, when you first came to Atlantis," said Noor, "you wondered why you were brought here. I said you came because of the prophecy but I did not know how you would help Atlantis. You did more than help. You saved Atlantis. Not by moving it, but by uniting the energy within it."

Adam felt a pleasant warmth suffuse his neck and cheeks.

"Destiny is the seed becoming a flower. Because you accepted your destiny, learned how to work with energy and became a part of the Three, the prophecy, although not fulfilled, still bloomed. Because you grew, we all benefitted."

I have super powers and I can do amazing things.

We have super powers and we do amazing things, Tya corrected him and she smiled the same little smile she had the first day he met her.

Adam blushed deeper. Had he projected the thought?

You're not so special, Earth Boy. I'm still better than you. One corner of Orri's mouth lifted.

The thirteen held hands in a circle around the table. A small spark of light shone in each of the thirteen skulls. The embers in the skulls grew until a soft radiance embraced the room.

"The power has begun." The deep voice of the thirteenth skull resonated around the council table.

"And with the power we will be," said Noor.

What's happening, Adam wondered.

No one said anything, and Adam didn't want to disturb the calm quietness. He looked around the table, enjoying the energy surging through his body. An unexpected feeling of homesickness flowed through him. He wondered how his family was.

Chapter Forty-Five

Adam's feet sank into the sand, and the granular particles squished between his toes. Looking down the beach, he saw the beautiful turquoise water lapping against the white sand. A heaviness filled his belly as he turned in a circle. What happened? How did I get here?

He kicked savagely at the sand. I didn't even get to say goodbye. He had left Atlantis the same way he entered it, with no warning or chance to change his mind. One minute he was there, and the next he was here. A tight band of sadness squeezed Adam's ribs. He pressed his palm to his chest to ease the sensation. His hand flattened against his t-shirt, and he realized his skull pendant was gone.

A warm vibration from the sand tickled the bottom of his feet. Adam drew the sensation from the soles of his feet, up his body and into his chest. Taking a deep breath, he enjoyed the familiar feeling. He grabbed a seashell off the beach and channeled all his energy into it. It didn't transform into a crystal like he intended. Without his skull pendant, he couldn't control the forces within him. He flung the shell out into the water.

Adam watched the waves as thoughts drifted through his mind. With or without his energy skills, he knew Atlantis existed. In another dimension, but still there. He knew he had a place there, just as he had a place here on Earth. But how to get from here to there and back again, he didn't know. And he didn't know how to fix it either, so for now he had to live with it.

Turning away from the water, he saw his dad walking toward him. Dad reminded him of James, and Adam wondered if he could find his birth father. He'd have to ask Mom and Dad about searching for him.

None of that mattered now. Thoughts of Atlantis dropped away. He was home! Running to his Dad, Adam threw his arms around him and squeezed tightly. "It's good to see you!"

His father hugged him, and then stepped back. "If a walk on the beach can change your attitude, maybe I should let you do it more often."

"I'd like that," said Adam.

Dad put his arm around Adam's shoulder. "The beach is a special place for you, isn't it?"

"Yeah, it really is." Maybe Dad understood after all.

As they walked down the beach together, Adam silently vowed to never forget Atlantis. No matter what happened, Noor, Orri, Tya, and all of them, even Cavan, would always be a part of him. And one day, he would go back.

THANK YOU FOR READING THIS BOOK

Without the support of readers like you, writers like me would not be able to write more books.

Buying books is the best way to support an author, but there are several other things you can do to help an author without spending any money:

1. Review the book on Amazon, Goodreads or anywhere the book is sold. Writing a review, especially if you have never written one, can be a difficult task. Most importantly, be honest. Then write a meaningful review, beyond "I loved it!" or "I didn't like it.", explain why the book caught your attention. If you are not sure how to phrase your comments look at other reviews for ideas.
2. Follow the author on social media.
3. Post about the book online.
4. Tell a friend (or 20) about the book.
5. Ask your local library to add the book to their collection.

ACKNOWLEDGMENTS

In our family, we say it takes a village to raise a child. This story has been my baby for a long time, and without the help of my writing village it would never have seen the light of day. This is my attempt to acknowledge all the people who have supported me in this endeavour.

To Dan, my husband, my muse, my alpha reader and my number one supporter. He looked at too many versions of this book to count and was always ready to read it again if I needed him to. Your love gives me the wings to make my dreams fly.

To Michell Plested who listened to my pitch and took me into Evil Alter Ego family. To editor Jeff Hite, for his amazing insight and Star Trek references. To Jeff Minkevics whose vision gave me an awesome cover. Without EAEP my vision would never have come true.

To my critique group, three women who took me into their fold, and showed me how to improve my writing in so many ways. I grew as a writer because of them.

To Sherry Brown, my friend and beta reader, her comments were not always easy to listen to but it was those observations I needed to hear the most.

To Susan Forest, my first editor who pushed my boundaries, told me to kill my darlings, and made me see how important plot was.

To the writing friends I have met along the way at classes, conferences, and places where writers meet. Sometimes a short conversation gave me the guts and understanding to keep moving forward.

There are so many people to thank, I know I will miss someone. So, if you have listened to me rattle on about my book, read dreadful early drafts, or have been a part of my life as I took this journey, you will never know how much you helped bring this story into the world.

ABOUT THE AUTHOR

J.M. Dover loves using both sides of her brain. Her past careers as a social worker, a fashion designer and an accountant prove she can be both creative and logical—sometimes strangely at the same time. Being a writer gives her a way where the two sides of her mind can play happily together.

She lives with her husband and requisite writers' pet (in this case, a loudly opinionated sheltie) in Calgary, Alberta.

Other Evil Alter Ego Press Books

The Fountain Series

The Fountain
By Suzy Vadori

The West Woods
By Suzy Vadori

Mik Murdoch: Boy Superhero Series

Mik Murdoch, Boy Superhero
By Michell Plested

Mik Murdoch: The Power Within
By Michell Plested

Mik Murdoch: Crisis of Conscience
By Michell Plested

Scouts of the Apocalypse Series

Scouts of the Apocalypse: Zombie Plague
By Michell Plested

Scouts of the Apocalypse: Zombie War
By Michell Plested

Anthologies

Dimensional Abscesses
(edited by Jeffrey Hite & Michell Plested)